D0359139

THE STRAYS

THE STRAYS

BARBARA LUDMAN

THOMAS NELSON INC., PUBLISHERS

Nashville, Tennessee / New York, New York

First edition

Library of Congress Cataloging in Publication Data

Ludman, Barbara.
    The strays.

    SUMMARY: A group of children in a quiet Florida town try to help
their friend whose father won't let her finish high school.

    [1. School stories] 1. Title.
PZ7.L9754St   [Fic]   76-19046
ISBN 0-8407-6503-7

For my mother
the Latin scholar

THE STRAYS

1

Strangers are rare in our part of Monroe, although they abound in the new developments. North Monroe, where the new houses are going up, is a lot like Miami, with people nobody ever saw before coming and going all the time.

Another rare phenomenon in Monroe is speeding trucks. Our town lies a good fifteen miles in from the highway, so the only trucks we ever see are short-haul carriers on their way to the supermarket, C. J. Caldwell's store and filling station, or the sprinkling of shops on Lee. Short-haul drivers tend to take their time.

That may explain why Alison Stewart and I stood motionless when we saw a speeding truck bearing down on a stranger crossing the road early one September morning.

Luckily, Ronnie Bean's bike had a flat tire. Ronnie was strolling along just ahead of us. His reaction time is legendary. Speedy reflexes and brains have made him a football great, despite his scrawny physique.

Quick as lightning, Ronnie spotted the truck, leaped into the road and tackled the stranger. The two of them landed in the gutter, while the truck squealed to a stop a few feet farther along. The driver leaned across the seat and stuck his head out the window.

"You kids okay?" he asked.

"Certainly," Ronnie said. "No thanks to you. I believe the speed limit in hick towns like this is twenty-five."

"Hippie," the driver growled. He shifted down with a mighty tear and drove on his way.

Ronnie was dusting himself off when Alison and I crossed the road. The stranger sprawled in the gutter, dazed. She was the palest sight I'd ever seen. Her hair was pale blond and her eyes were pale blue. Even her dress was pale, an old, faded blue dress with bouquets of pink flowers. It billowed out unevenly in the gutter.

"Did I break anything?" Ronnie asked her.

She sat up against the curb. "Hey," she said slowly. "You saved my life."

"I suppose I did," Ronnie agreed.

"It was spectacular," I remarked.

Ronnie ignored me.

"I believe that among the Japanese," he said to no one in particular, "when one person saves another person's life, that person is the person's slave for life."

"Which person?" I asked, confused.

"The savee, of course," Ronnie said. "The savee owes her life to the saver. She's got to do as he orders. I've got a couple of ideas. . . ."

"You've got it wrong," Alison broke in, exasperated. "It's the other way around. You've got to be her slave." She turned her back on Ronnie. "How do you do," she said to the stranger. "I'm Alison Stewart."

"Stella Shanks," the stranger said. "Y'all sure got a lot of fast traffic here."

"It's very unusual," Alison assured her.

"That doesn't make any sense," Ronnie said. "Why should I be her slave? I saved her life."

"When Stella walked in front of that truck, she gave you a chance to do a good deed," Alison explained. "You should be grateful to her. It's done your karma a lot of good."

10

Ronnie glowered at Alison. "Are you sure? Anyway," he went on, "we're not in Japan. Now in Monroe . . ."

"In Monroe," Alison pointed out, "slavery is out of fashion. The last slave in Monroe was my great-great-grandmother's second cousin."

"I believe there were never any slaves in Monroe," Ronnie said. "We're too far south."

I decided to step in quickly. Ronnie and Alison are both rather bright, and sometimes their intellectual rivalry gets out of hand.

"Do you really care about our local history?" I asked Stella.

Stella never had a chance. Ronnie is hard to stop when once he seizes on a subject.

"Monroe may not look like a big city," he said, stating the obvious, "but you'd be surprised how big it is. We have five thousand inhabitants, representing every race and creed."

"Not every race and creed," Alison interrupted. "There are no Japanese people here yet. Lucky for you, the way you invent Japanese customs."

"I stand corrected," Ronnie said. "Alison represents the black community."

"Represents?" Alison laughed. "I *am* the black community."

Ronnie ignored her. "I represent that brave and intrepid band of poor, ignorant white folk who crawled out of the swamps around the turn of the century to clear a few square miles of wilderness and farm the rich Florida soil. Now Mary Frances," he continued, waving an arm in my direction, "Mary Frances represents the Yankee carpetbaggers. Wasn't it your grandparents who came down here from Cleveland, Ohio?"

"My great-great-grandmother's second cousin," I said, disgusted. I turned to Stella. "Are you on your way to school, by any chance?"

"I think so," Stella said uncertainly. "Am I headed right?"

"You can walk along with us," I said. "We're going that way."

We must have made an odd-looking assortment hurrying down the road on that sunny September morning. We looked as different as three girls can possibly look. Alison—blue-black, tall and long-legged, her hair cut short as a cap—set a rapid pace. I'm possibly the shortest person in Monroe, and I took three steps to two of Alison's trying to keep up, my long, brown hair falling into my eyes. Stella, who was of a size and shape the critical ladies of Monroe would consider "just right," walked between us, holding to a steady pace. We must have looked like a set of steep bobbing steps to Ronnie, who took pains to lag behind us.

"I bet you got a fine school," Stella said after we'd covered half a block.

"It's pretty ordinary," I said. "Just a bunch of rooms and desks."

"How many rooms y'all got?" Stella asked.

Alison and I looked at each other. "Ten?" Alison ventured. "Fifteen?"

Stella stopped short, and we stopped with her. "Fifteen!" she said. "We ain't got but two where I come from."

Ronnie found the conversation so interesting that he caught up with us. "Did you actually go to a two-room school, Stella?" he asked. "I didn't believe they still existed."

"I'm here to tell you," Stella replied. "Fifteen rooms! Man! You got a gym?"

"Well, yes," Ronnie admitted. "You'd have to count that as one of the rooms. Fourteen rooms and a gym. Not very big, really."

"Man!" Stella said. "Sounds big to me. I just knew a fine city like this would have a fine school to go with it." She thought a moment. "You got an assembly hall?"

We were deep in conversation when George Harris jogged

past. His head jerked in our direction and his long red ponytail whipped around and hit him in the mouth. Without breaking stride, he turned around and jogged back. I don't know why George jogs all the time. Alison says he does it to improve his image. It makes him look like an athlete, she says.

Poor George. He's bigger than Ronnie, but he's not well coordinated. After three years of jogging everywhere, he's only managed to make second-string alternate offensive tackle. We think the coach took pity on him because he's Ronnie's friend.

George greeted Alison, me, and Ronnie, in that order, because he's very polite. Then he stared at Stella.

I introduced them.

"Welcome to Monroe," George boomed.

Stella beamed. "This here sure looks like a fine city."

The five of us spread across the sidewalk and ambled along for another block. Then we heard Stella draw in her breath.

"Well, just look at that."

We'd reached the school.

Monroe School seemed to live up to Stella's high expectations. She told us that where she came from, the town hall wasn't as big as our school building. The grass was the finest, greenest grass she'd ever seen; the frangipani trees scattered around the grounds were really fine frangipanis; the gravel walks were the finest gravel walks in the state of Florida.

We tend to be modest in Monroe. Dad says we've got plenty to be modest about. Monroe's a backwater, he says, tucked miles away from the coast and pretty far south of the orange groves, where nobody would ever notice us. Progress has passed us by without so much as a glance.

I suppose Dad's right. Compared with Miami, we might as well be on the moon. Anyway, Ronnie and George seemed to be modest enough, because Stella's enthusiasm was embarrassing them. I decided to get her onto another subject.

"When did you go to a two-room school?" I asked Stella.

"Last year," she said. "We went in shifts. Hey. Y'all don't go to school in shifts?"

I looked at Alison, who looked at George, who looked at Ronnie, who looked back at me. We'd never heard of shifts.

"Y'all don't talk much," Stella said. "I bet you got real fine classrooms. Which way do we go?"

The first day of every school year is pretty boring because it's given over to organization. The teacher feels called upon to welcome us back to school and tell us how much we're going to learn this year. Then she calls our names in alphabetical order, and she tells us where to sit.

The first person called always sits in the first seat by the door; the second person sits in the next one back; and so on. That's supposed to be democratic.

Our teacher that year was Miss Holloway. She'd been in Monroe for a couple of years—long enough to get through her welcoming speech without too much trouble. That chore over, she began to call the roll. I was stuck in the front row; my name is always called first. For years, I'd hoped some day a new kid would arrive with a name like Aardvark or maybe Alabaster, anything before Allen. It hasn't happened yet.

Stella wasn't any too pleased with her seat, either. It was in the last row. Stella looked at her assigned desk with dismay.

"Can't I have a seat in the front, ma'am?" she asked.

A few people laughed. They thought it was a joke. So did Miss Holloway. "That will do, Stella," she said. "Just take your seat."

Stella walked slowly to the back of the room.

I glanced back at her once or twice that first morning. She was toying with a pencil, looking fit to be tied.

When the bell rang for lunch, Stella was the last person to file out of the room. I waited for her.

"Want to see the lunchroom?"

14

Stella cheered up. "Hey," she said. "You got a lunchroom?" Then she looked downcast. "I don't have nothing to eat."

"That's okay," I assured her. "You can buy something there."

"That depends," she said. "What can I get for a dime?"

"You only have a dime?" I said, amazed. "Don't you have an allowance?"

"Sure. A dime a day. How much y'all get around here?"

"It depends." I knew the line would be winding out past the lunchroom door if we dallied much longer. "I'll lend you some money," I offered.

"Can't pay you back," Stella said sadly. "I never have any money."

"I'll give you some money," I said, getting exasperated.

"Can't I buy anything for a dime?"

"Let's see." I started to walk to the lunchroom. To my relief, Stella followed. "A brownie's fifteen cents. There's potato chips. Hamburgers are twenty cents. Wait a minute. Milk."

"Milk's a dime?"

"Milk's free," I said. "All you can drink."

Stella smiled. "I'm suddenly so hungry I can barely stand it," she said. We speeded up.

The line was winding out past the lunchroom door. We fell in at the end of it, and Stella started to tell me about her desk.

"I got to find me a way to get a desk in the front row," she said.

"Why?"

"It's hard to explain."

I looked for somebody to let us in at the front of the line. There wasn't anybody.

"Last year I went to a school that was so old and crummy there were holes in the wall," she said suddenly. "I sat in the back row, just like I am now. We had to go to school in

15

shifts. I went in the afternoon shift, and I used to look through the holes in the wall and see the flowers growing and the birds flying and the kids from the morning shift kicking a ball around. All I learned all year was George Washington was the first President, and I already knew that."

"I don't think I'd mind that at all," I said.

Stella acted as if she hadn't heard me. "All my schools were pretty bad," she went on. "We move around a lot. This here looks like a fine school. I think I can learn something. I don't want to be stuck away in the back of the room. The teacher might say something real important and I could miss it." She grinned. "She might even say the name of the second President."

"She hasn't yet, anyway," I said. "Teachers here don't seem too interested in the federal system. They concentrate mostly on the Confederacy."

"I don't mind," Stella said. "I'll learn about anything. How to talk good and how to do algebra. There don't seem to be much they can teach me that I already know."

We each took a tray and walked along the cafeteria counter. I bought a hamburger at the hot table; Stella set two glasses of milk on her tray. We slid our trays off the counter and stood there a moment.

I spotted Ronnie at a long, half-empty table.

"Come on," I said. "Follow me."

Ronnie's face fell when he noticed me bearing down on him. I sat next to him anyway.

"Sit down, Stella," I said. "Don't pay any attention to Ronnie."

"Thanks," said Ronnie. "You flatter me."

"We need a plan," I said.

"What kind of a plan?" he asked, casually. I knew he'd be interested; Ronnie was a great planner.

16

"Stella wants to sit in the front of the class."

"She can have your seat."

"I don't think Miss Holloway will approve that arrangement," I said. "She'll probably think I want to sit in the back."

"You do."

"It wouldn't upset me a lot," I admitted.

"How about glasses, Stella?" Ronnie asked. "Do you wear glasses?"

"Nope."

"Do you know anybody who wears glasses?"

"No."

Ronnie looked disappointed. He drank some milk.

"Know anybody who has a hearing aid?"

"My granddaddy."

"Can you get hold of it?"

"I guess he'd give it to me if I asked."

"Good," Ronnie said. "Now here's the plan."

The rest of the day passed without incident. I had to stay after school to sign up for the school choir. When I had finished the formalities, Stella was gone, so I had no chance to discuss Ronnie's plan with her.

But the next morning, I knew she'd decided to go through with it. When I walked into the classroom, there was Stella, seated at her assigned desk, wearing a piece of plastic on her ear.

She'd pulled her hair back to make the hearing aid more evident and she kept poking at it. Ronnie turned around and scowled at her, so she stopped.

Miss Holloway didn't notice a thing when she arrived a few minutes later. She was nearly through calling the roll when it happened.

"Stella Shanks," she said.

There was no response. Miss Holloway looked up.

"Stella?" she said again.

Stella leaped to her feet. "Sorry, ma'am," she said. "I couldn't hear you. Didn't have my hearing aid turned on high enough."

"Hearing aid?" Miss Holloway said. "Is that a hearing aid?"

"Yes, ma'am. 'Course it breaks down sometimes and then I can't hear a thing."

Right on schedule, the hearing aid started to whine. Stella looked startled. So was I. That wasn't part of the plan.

Stella took the hearing aid off and started to fiddle with it. The whine reached ear-shattering proportions.

"Bring it to me, please," Miss Holloway said over the din.

Stella marched up to the front of the room and laid the hearing aid on Miss Holloway's desk.

"You can sit down now," Miss Holloway said, and she examined the hearing aid while Stella walked back to her desk.

Miss Holloway turned a knob and the sound cut off in midwhine.

"Nothing the matter with this," Miss Holloway muttered. "Just inexperience." And in the same mutter, she added, "You may pick it up now, Stella."

Stella leaped to her feet and started down the aisle. Miss Holloway's next words froze her in her tracks.

"You could hear that, could you, from the back of the room? I suppose you'll say you were reading my lips."

"Yes, ma'am," Stella said hopefully.

Miss Holloway mouthed a few syllables. Then she asked, "What did I say?"

"Come up to the desk?" Stella ventured. Miss Holloway's face tightened up. "Go back to my seat?" Miss Holloway's face grew even tighter.

18

Stella grinned. "Get on home?" A few people tittered. Stella was getting reckless now. "Go climb a tree?" She started to laugh and the class broke up. We were roaring when Miss Holloway's voice broke through.

"I said, 'I doubt that very much,' " she replied. "You're no more deaf than I am. You may return to your seat, Stella. I'll just keep this hearing aid for a while. You may pick it up after school."

I heard the outcome of Stella's after-school talk with Miss Holloway from Ronnie, who stayed behind to listen at the door. I guess he felt responsible—or maybe just curious.

Miss Holloway began the discussion.

"It's a sin to tell a lie," she said.

Stella acknowledged that was so.

"If you know that," Miss Holloway asked, "why did you do it?"

"I wanted to sit in the front row, ma'am," Stella replied.

"We can't always have everything we want."

Stella acknowledged that was so.

"It won't affect my decision," Miss Holloway went on, "but I'm puzzled. Was there some compelling reason why you wanted to sit in the front row?"

"I don't know how compelling it is, ma'am," Stella replied, "but I had a reason." Then she told Miss Holloway what she had told me the day before. Stella told her about her last school, and the afternoon shift, and the holes in the wall. She explained how much she wanted to learn, now that she had the chance to go to a fine school like this one.

Ronnie said Miss Holloway was quiet for long afterward. It made him nervous, and he started to move away from the door. Then suddenly she spoke.

"That certainly sounds like a compelling reason," she said. "But the law is the law. We cannot make an exception to the seating rule, however compelling your reason may be."

19

Stella said she understood.

"I'm going to have to punish you for lying and creating a disturbance in the classroom," Miss Holloway went on. "Take a piece of chalk. No, the long one. Now write on the blackboard: 'I will be honest.' "

Ronnie said he supposed she wrote it, because he heard the chalk scratching. When it stopped, he heard Miss Holloway say, "They certainly haven't taught you penmanship. You will stay after school every day for an hour and write that sentence again and again, until you can write it so that someone can read it. Try it again."

That's when Ronnie left.

I spotted Stella walking down the road after school one day a week later.

"Hey, wait a minute," I yelled, pulling up. "Which way are you walking?"

"Up to Second Street. That's where I live."

"Nobody lives on Second Street," I said, and then I was sorry I'd said it.

Second Street is a run-down street stuck smack in the middle of an ordinary residential neighborhood. There's a big ditch on Second Street, and people used to throw their trash into it until the City Council said they had to stop. People say it smells bad anyway. There's nothing there but a couple of vacant lots, C.J. Caldwell's store and filling station, and an old abandoned wooden house.

"You live in that old house?" I asked her finally.

"I don't live at C.J.'s," she retorted. "Where do you live?"

"Poinsettia Street. It's just a couple of blocks past your street. Like to come by?"

"Can't. I got to go home and do my homework." Stella grinned. "I lost a lot of time learning how to be honest."

We walked along for a bit in silence.

"I can stop at C.J.'s for an orange soda," Stella suggested. I agreed.

C.J. was sitting out on a rickety wooden bench in front of the store, a great, fat mountain of a man with a bottle of beer in his hand. He frowned when he saw us.

"What you kids want?"

"Soda," Stella answered.

C.J. tipped back his head, finished his beer, straightened up, and threw the bottle into a big empty lard can set out next to the bench. He belched. Then he looked at us again.

"Go on, git inside," he growled. "The missus'll git you what you want."

We walked past C.J. into the store. C.J.'s wife was leaning on the counter, and she smiled when she saw us.

"Well, good afternoon," she said. "Stella, Mary Frances. Something you ladies want?"

"Two orange sodas, please, ma'am," Stella answered.

Mrs. C.J. straightened up. "Coming right up," she said.

"That's okay, ma'am, we can get them," I said. I walked over to the cold case to fetch the sodas and saw my six-year-old brother sitting on the floor.

"Hey, Pete," I said. "What are you doing sitting on the floor behind the cold case?"

Pete muttered something I didn't get.

"What's that?"

Pete shot me a glower and went on staring at a spot on the wall. I decided not to question him any further. Pete likes to keep to himself.

I pulled out the sodas and snapped off the tops. Then I leaned over the case very quietly to see what Pete was up to. After a moment or two a mouse scuttled by. I wasn't surprised. C.J.'s is the kind of store a mouse would like: cool and dark and dusty.

The mouse stopped just opposite Pete, wrinkled its nose at him once or twice, and then scurried out of sight.

I decided I'd better do the same. Pete didn't like to share his secrets. I got back to the counter just in time to see Pete run past and out the door, waving his arms and grinning like a fool.

Stella and Mrs. C.J. were deep in conversation.

"So you finished learning to be honest, Stella?" Mrs. C.J. asked.

"Yes, ma'am," Stella said. "I sure write a nice hand now. Like to see?"

"Sure would," Mrs. C.J. said. She handed Stella a piece of paper bag and the stubby pencil she used to add up prices.

Stella wrote "I will be honest." I have to admit it looked good. She wrote a nice, round hand.

Mrs. C.J. was impressed. "I think Emily ought to see this," she said. "Emily!" she called.

Emily came out of the back room, her usual haunt at this time of day. Most days I could hear her mumbling over her homework. Emily was a senior in high school and she studied practically all the time. We figured she was smarter than most of the teachers.

"Let me see," Emily said, taking the scrap of paper bag to study. "That's good, Stella," she said finally. "Now let's see you write something else."

She pondered for a moment. "How about 'My life closed twice before its close—/ It yet remains to see/ If Immortality unveil/ A third event to me.'"

Stella stared at her. "I don't even know what that means," she said.

"It's from a poem by Emily Dickinson," Emily explained. "She was a major American poet about a hundred years ago."

"Emily's called after her," Mrs. C.J. said. "I used to love hearing her poems. 'So huge, so hopeless to conceive/ As these that twice befell./ Parting is all we know of heaven,/ And all we need of hell.' That's the rest of the poem," she explained, as Stella and I stood openmouthed.

Dad says one of the problems of small-town life is that everybody has a role to play. The Caldwell family usually played its role well. C.J. was always half drunk and nasty.

Emily always had her freckled nose stuck in a book. And Mrs. C.J.—well, Mrs. C.J. usually played her role of a simple, good-natured, uneducated lady to the hilt. I'd never heard Mrs. C.J. quote poetry before, and I doubt whether anyone but Emily had either. I was fascinated by this new side of her.

"That's wonderful," I said finally.

"Why don't you try the last two lines, Stella?" Emily suggested. " 'Parting is all we know of heaven,/ And all we need of hell.' "

Stella had barely put stubby pencil to paper bag when we heard C.J. yelling from his bench:

"Callie!"

Mrs. C.J. looked up, startled. Then she halloed back.

"Git me a beer!" C.J. yelled.

Mrs. C.J. straightened up and started to walk over to the cold case. Suddenly she stopped and sat on a box. We all looked at her. She had turned very pale.

"I'm feeling dizzy," she explained, looking embarrassed.

Briskly, Emily fetched the beer, opened it, and carried it out to her father.

"Something we can do, ma'am?" Stella wanted to know.

"Oh, no, Stella, you're a good girl," Mrs. C.J. said, resting on the box. "I'll be fine in a minute. It just comes over me sometimes."

Emily returned as briskly as she'd parted. "Let's see what you've written, Stella."

"Oh, that's okay," Stella said. "Got to get home now."

But Emily was stubborn. "It won't take more than three minutes," she said. "Try it. 'Parting is all we know of heaven,/ And all we need of hell.' " She smiled suddenly. "It's good for the soul."

Mrs. C.J. returned to the counter while Stella was writing. She was still pale. But when Stella had finished, she wanted to see what she had written. Emily showed it to her.

"Now that's a nice hand," Mrs. C.J. said. "Ain't that a nice hand, Emily?"

"It's very good," Emily said. "Just keep it up." She smiled at us and returned to the back room.

Stella reached into her pocket. "Got to get home now, ma'am," she said, pulling out a dime. I paid for my soda too and we left. As we walked past C.J. he scowled at us, and then he belched.

"He sure likes his beer," Stella whispered.

We stopped just past the gas pump, where C.J. couldn't hear us.

"That's just in the daytime," I told her. "He starts drinking whiskey after five o'clock."

"I knew a man once just like that," Stella said. "He was big and fat and he drank whiskey all the time. He got to seeing things. Once—"

"What kind of things?" I interrupted.

"Ghosts, mainly," Stella explained, "and flying animals. Once he saw a camel. Now I can tell you they don't have no camels up in north Florida. One time he saw an eagle flying over his house with a Christmas tree in its claws, all lit up with a star on top. One night he saw the devil."

"No!" I exclaimed.

"Well, he thought he did. So he thought, why, he'd make the devil feel at home, and he set fire to his house. Burned down to the ground," she went on sadly. "The whole family had to sleep down on the riverbank until winter, out in the rain."

"Did they ever get another house?"

"I don't know," she said. "We moved."

I saw the blond boy before Stella did. He was about eighteen or nineteen, with long straight hair pulled back, and eyes so blue I noticed them when he was twenty yards away. He walked in a wide circle to avoid us and strolled over to

C.J. They said a few words to one another and then the boy sat down on the bench.

"Callie!" C.J. yelled.

Stella looked up and saw the boy.

Her face changed. "Got to get home," she said suddenly. She turned off to the right.

I walked on a bit and then looked back. Mrs. C.J. was handing the boy a can of beer.

I turned homeward, but I couldn't stop thinking about the boy I'd seen sitting out with C.J., a beer in his hand. C.J. had always had a steady stream of visitors, but most of them were middle-aged men like himself. They'd sidle up to that rickety wooden bench, shake C.J.'s hand, sit a while, drink a beer, and then sidle off the way they'd come.

I'd seen a lot of middle-aged men sharing C.J.'s bench over the years, but I'd never seen a boy there before. C.J. had never tolerated kids. He didn't even like Emily, and she was his own daughter.

I was thinking that nobody in our small town was sticking to his role today when Ronnie sped by on his bike.

"Hey, Mary Frances," he yelled. "I'm coming to see your dogs."

"Practice called off?" I yelled back.

Ronnie coasted to a stop. "A bit early in the season."

"Okay," I said. "Is George coming too?"

"I expect him any minute."

I drew level with him, and we began walking along to my house.

"Hey," I said. "Just now. Did you see that boy with C.J.?"

"I may have noticed him."

"Ever see him before?"

"Don't think so."

"Funny thing," I said, "but Stella seemed scared of him."

"I'm not surprised. He looks like a hood."

26

"What gives you that idea?"

"I've been around," he said.

"Where?"

"Never mind."

We walked along in silence.

"I thought he looked kind of interesting," I remarked finally.

Ronnie stopped short. I stopped with him. "That's just the kind of remark I'd expect from somebody as inexperienced as you are," he said angrily. "You wouldn't know a hood from a preacher." He grabbed my arm and stared into my face. "Listen, Mary Frances, just listen to me. Don't start hanging around C.J.'s and talking to anybody who comes along."

"I wasn't planning to," I retorted hotly.

Ronnie gazed at me a moment longer, then dropped my arm. We proceeded to my house in silence.

Scrappy started to bark as soon as Ronnie wheeled his bike onto the gravel driveway.

"Who's that?"

"That's a new one," I told him. "His name's Scrappy. He's a little nervous."

"How long have you had him?"

"About a week. I don't think he's used to all the other dogs. Mom thinks he must have had a hard time before he got here, because he's so jumpy."

Ronnie leaned his bike against the garage. We opened the gate and all the dogs began to bark, together.

We have nine of them. The oldest one is Doggo, a big, hairy white dog who sleeps all the time. He must be very old by now. He was getting on when we found him, and that was years ago.

I remember the day Doggo started hanging around the house. In fact, I was the one who found him. I spotted him early in the afternoon, lying in the shade of the frangipani.

It was a hot, bright, sunny afternoon late in June, and Mom went out to give him a bowl of water. He drank it in one gulp and started to follow us back into the house.

"Go home," Mom said.

The dog didn't move.

"Go home," Mom said again, and hustled me inside the house.

The dog sat on the front steps.

He sat there all afternoon. When the sun went down, Mom and I gave him something to eat. That's when we noticed he didn't have a collar.

"I expect somebody's looking for this dog," Mom said. "Better call the newspaper."

We called the newspaper, the radio station, the police, and the animal shelter. The police and the people at the shelter assured us that nobody was looking for a big white dog.

The newspaper published our classified advertisement the next day and Doggo's description was broadcast over the radio four or five times. But nobody came to claim him.

"Funny," Mom said.

I didn't mind. I was getting used to having Doggo around. He spent most of the time lying under the frangipani, day and night.

The problem of Doggo grew serious a week later. Every July we drove south to Miami for two weeks, and it was drawing near to our annual departure time.

"I think we'd better postpone our vacation," Dad said on the last day of June.

"We can't," Mom said. "Your mother will be so disappointed. You know how she looks forward to these visits."

"We'll have to find someone to look after Doggo, then."

Mom was silent for a while. Then she said, "Perhaps we'd better take him to the shelter."

"That's not a very good idea," said Dad.

"Why not? They'll take good care of him there, and maybe somebody will adopt him."

Dad didn't argue. "We'll see."

The day before we were due to leave on vacation, we all piled into the car and drove to the shelter. It was a big stone building without any windows, like a tiny fort. We left Pete, who was still a fat, dribbly baby in those days, leaning against Doggo in the back seat of the car.

Mom looked uneasy as soon as we entered the shelter. "I don't like it," she said. "It shouldn't smell like this. Don't they ever clean it?"

The woman in charge asked us if we wanted to adopt a dog.

"Actually," my father said, "we were hoping to leave one with you."

"Not another one! We're full up. We have to take it, of course," she relented grimly. "That's the law. But look at this."

She took us down a dark hall and opened a door. I couldn't believe it. The walls were lined with wire cages, and there were two or three dogs in every cage. The smell was terrible.

"Don't you ever clean this room?" my mother demanded.

"Clean it!" the woman snorted. "It's all we can do to get these dogs walked and fed. They haven't got a chance, poor things. Nobody's going to adopt a full-grown dog. Come with me." She walked out of the room.

We followed the woman down another passage, and she opened another door. It was a small room and there were puppies everywhere, flopped atop each other.

"This is what people adopt," she said. "Cute little puppies. Some of them were born here."

We walked out and headed toward the entrance.

"What's going to happen to those dogs?" Mom asked the woman.

"The puppies? Most of them will be adopted."

"Not the puppies. The older dogs."

The woman was silent.

"Well?" Mom said.

"You see our problem," the woman answered. "People adopt a cute little puppy, and it grows up to be a big dog, and they bring it back. Or they just leave it in the street. Or it's hard to house-train; it piddles all over their living-room carpet. So they bring it to us. And we don't have any room. We have to put the dogs to sleep."

"How?" I asked.

Everybody looked at me. "Don't be morbid," Dad said sharply.

"Do you shoot them?"

"Of course not," the woman said angrily. "We're thoroughly modern. We've got a small room fitted up with an efficient machine that pumps all the air out."

Now my mother was angry too. "How can you do such a wicked thing?" she said, her voice shaking.

"Now, Margaret, calm down," said Dad.

"It's fast and painless and they don't know a thing," the woman said defensively. "They die in their sleep."

"It's sheer wickedness!" Mom cried.

"If you feel so strongly about it, why don't you adopt a dog? I have a dog here nobody will ever want. He's five years old and he's sick. He piddles everywhere. He can't control himself. We'll probably put him to sleep tomorrow."

Mom was enraged. "Of course, we'll adopt him!" she cried.

"But, Margaret," Dad said. "What about the new living-room carpet?"

"We'll take him!" Mom said. Dad grinned.

The woman disappeared again and returned with a large brown dachshund with a wart on his nose. "His name is Persimmon," she said.

"Persimmon!" Dad said. "No wonder he's sick." He tickled the dog under the chin. "Don't worry, old fellow. We can do better than that."

The woman handed Mom the dog. "Just fill out the form," she told Dad, "and he's all yours."

"Did you take him to a veterinarian?" Mom asked, calmer now.

"What for?" the woman asked. "It may sound callous, but we need the money we have to take care of the dogs someone is going to adopt. I don't know what's wrong with him. You might ask the people who left him with us. They said he was beginning to be too much trouble."

My mother gasped. I thought she was shocked at the callous attitude of the dog's previous owners, and maybe she was. But the dog had just piddled all over Mom's dress.

The woman smiled. "We won't take him back, you know," she said.

"We won't bring him back," Mom said. "I'd like to save all of them," she added extravagantly.

"At least," Dad said, handing back the form, "we can save one."

That was the beginning of our kennel. We marched out to the car with Percy, plonked him between Pete and Doggo, and drove to the office of Dr. Robinson, the only veterinarian in Monroe. Dr. Robinson examined Percy and gave us some pills to hide in his food. Percy was cured within a week. There was no vacation that year, but nobody minded very much.

Percy was followed by a host of dogs over the years. We took what Dad called "hard-core cases": the dogs nobody else wanted.

A fat and elderly Percy came waddling up to the gate when Ronnie and I opened it. He wagged his tail once or twice, then waddled back to flop down next to Doggo.

31

Ronnie threw a few sticks for the dogs to fetch, shadow-boxed with two of the younger dogs, and patted the rest. Then he pulled a handful of dog biscuits out of his back pocket.

"I only brought eight," he said apologetically. "I didn't know you had a new one."

"That's all right," I said. "Scrappy wouldn't eat it anyway. The other dogs wouldn't let him."

Ronnie was shocked. "Why not?"

"Maybe they know how jumpy he is," I said. "They never let him eat with them. They eat all his food. I have to feed him in the kitchen."

Ronnie broke one of the biscuits in half. "Old Percy won't mind," he said, giving one half to the dachshund. He distributed the rest of the biscuits and then opened the door to the kitchen. "Come on, Scrappy," he said.

Scrappy stood immobile.

"I don't think he knows his name yet," I said. I grabbed his collar and pulled him into the kitchen. We closed the screen door and Ronnie held out the half biscuit.

Scrappy examined the kitchen very carefully. Satisfied, he sat, looking peaceful. Suddenly he leaped up and grabbed the biscuit. He ate it quickly, growling, in a corner. When he'd finished, we let him back out into the yard.

Scrappy had just flopped down a few feet past Doggo and Percy when George jogged through the gate, waving a math book.

"Hey, Mary Frances," he said. "Hey, Ronnie. There's something in this book I don't understand."

There's nothing in the math book I understand, so I was perfectly willing to hang around while Ronnie explained algebra to George. We three settled in at the kitchen table.

Pete barreled in ten minutes later, wearing a football helmet. He looked neither right nor left but went straight to the cupboard.

"How's tricks, Pete?" Ronnie said.

Pete didn't pay any· attention. He grabbed a couple of Oreos and barreled out, slamming the screen door.

Ronnie looked at me. "Strange kid," he said.

"Well," I replied, "he kind of keeps his own counsel."

George looked puzzled. "What does that mean?"

"I don't know," I answered honestly, and we returned to the open math book.

A lot of families eat dinner in silence, or even separately. But Dad says it's the only time he has a chance to see us, so he's set certain rules. Dinner begins at six, and Pete and I have to be there.

Nobody expects Pete to say much, but I'm required to converse. I'm supposed to keep the conversation on an adult level; I'm not quite sure what that is.

"You know Stella?" I asked my family in general that night at dinner.

"Is that the little girl who got into trouble over a hearing aid?" Mom asked.

"That's the one," I said, grinning. "Actually, it was Ronnie's idea."

"I'm not surprised," Mom said. She laughed.

My father looked up from his meat loaf. "What's this?"

I recounted the episode of the hearing aid. Dad laughed.

"So that's what you children get up to when you're supposed to be learning something."

"Stella learned something from it," I said. "She learned to write real good."

"Real well," Mom said absently. Mom teaches English in the high school.

"Real well," I repeated. "We were over at C.J.'s today and she gave us a sample."

"What were you doing at C.J.'s?" Mom wanted to know.

33

"Drinking Nehi, I expect," Dad said.

"Actually it was orange soda."

"Whatever it was," Dad said, growing stern, "I hope you're not going to make a habit of it. I don't hold with children spending the afternoon in places like that."

Pete looked up suddenly, and then looked back at his plate.

"Stella lives down Second Street," I said, trying to keep the conversation on an adult level.

"Not in that old house!" Mom cried.

"That's what she said. She's real friendly with Mrs. C.J."

"Well, Callie's all right," Mom said. "The poor woman. But her husband is a sorry specimen indeed."

Dad spoke up in C.J.'s defense. "The store used to be reasonably successful," he pointed out. "It isn't easy these days to make a store like that pay. There was a time he employed sound business practices."

Dad owns a men's shop over on Lee, and he has a high regard for sound business practices.

"But he's let it all slip now," Dad continued. "He was decent enough before the oil company offered him a gasoline franchise. I'm afraid it's gone to his head."

Mom doesn't put too much stock in sound business practices. "C.J.'s always been lazy and shiftless," she said, getting straight to the point. "He's stupid and prejudiced as well."

"You should have seen him today," I said. "He was drinking beer out on that crummy bench. I guess he was minding the gas pump. In case a big truck happened to come along and want gas at a dollar a gallon. Mrs. C.J. had a dizzy spell."

"You're turning into a regular old gossip," Dad said. "What's for dessert?"

Dad returned to the subject of C.J.'s over the chocolate cake.

"I think you have more important things to do with your time," he said, "than to spend it at C.J.'s."

"Okay," I said. "You're the boss."

"Childhood is short enough," Dad said, and the subject was closed.

3

My father's warning wasn't really necessary. What with one thing and another, I'd never spent a lot of time at C.J.'s.

One thing was choir practice once a week. I sing alto, and although my voice isn't very pretty, it's strong. Miss Jones, the music teacher, says I carry a heavy responsibility, because I'm the only alto who can read music. If I miss choir practice, the altos won't know how the tune goes. I joined the choir when I was in the second grade, and I've always believed it was a serious mistake, because now Miss Jones won't let me quit.

Another reason I don't spend much time at C.J.'s is Alison. She's my closest friend, and she won't set foot in the place.

Stella found that out one Friday a week or two later. The three of us had left together after school for my house.

"Hey," Stella said, as we neared Second Street. "Want to go to C.J.'s for an orange soda?"

"I don't think we'd better," I said.

"Why not?" said Stella.

"Alison doesn't like it."

"Why not?"

"It's dirty," Alison said. "And C.J.'s prejudiced."

Stella was a little slow to understand. "It's the law now," she said. "Don't matter how prejudiced he is. He has to let you buy an orange soda."

"Do you know," Alison said, "when I was small, we had to

go all the way across town to buy our food, because C.J. wouldn't serve us. 'Don't have to,' he told us. 'Got enough business without nigger trade.' Well, now there's the super-market, and we don't need C.J. I wouldn't give that man any of my money."

"I don't think he's got nothing against you personally," Stella said. "He just don't like nobody. You should hear the things he yells at poor George Harris. George just has to jog by, and C.J. yells, 'Hey, stupid' or 'Gonna make the girls softball team?' Something dumb like that. C.J., he don't like Catholics, or Jews, or Chinese, or foreigners, or even people from Miami."

"That's his loss," Alison said haughtily. We marched past C.J.'s, our heads high. We had just crossed the street when Stella stopped.

"Anyway," she said suddenly, "I got to go home for a minute. Wait here."

She walked five steps up Second Street, stopped, and came back.

"Like to come over for a minute?" she asked.

We accepted the invitation. And I understood Stella's hesitation about inviting us to her house as soon as we opened the screen door to the sun porch.

Nobody had lived in that house for years. Nobody had painted it or fixed the broken windows or even swept the floor. The porch screens were torn. Pushed against the wall was an old couch, its stuffing coming out in half a dozen places.

Alison and I were too embarrassed to say anything. We walked through the desolation as if we saw it every day of our lives.

"Can't offer you nothing to eat," Stella said cheerfully. "Nobody's home and there's nothing in the Frigidaire."

We followed her through a long, dark hall. Paint was peeling off the walls and there were great gray blotches everywhere. Stella turned into the second room on the right and we followed.

I don't want to give the impression that the room was the light and airy bedroom of a princess. But compared with what we'd just seen, for a moment I thought maybe it was. The room was clean and newly painted yellow. A neatly made cot was set out in the middle, and a rickety little table and a dresser, all brand new and shining. There was even a picture on the wall, an unframed poster of sunflowers.

"What a pretty room," Alison said.

Stella looked critically around her. "It's not bad," she said. "My brother fixed it up. I'd show you his room too, but he don't like people poking around his life."

"I didn't know you had a brother," I said.

"Yeah," Stella admitted.

"How old is he?"

"Older than me," Stella said, dropping her books on the dresser. "You never saw him." She opened the top drawer, took out a dollar and stuffed it into the pocket of her dress.

"Got to buy food for dinner," she said. "My mama's got a job, working nights."

"Does she let you buy the food?" Alison asked. She sounded a little envious.

"Don't have nothing to say about it," Stella said, walking out of the room. "My granddaddy's gone back to Atlanta. My brother runs the family now." She grinned. "I got to account to him for every penny I spend."

We filed out of the room and started down the dark hall. I glanced into the room next to Stella's and stopped short.

"Hey, Stella," I said. "Is this your brother's room?"

Even while I asked, I knew it couldn't be. It was the most

extraordinary room I had ever seen. Nearly everything in it was red. There was a red bedspread on the big brass bed, and red curtains hanging on the windows, and a big fluffy red scatter rug on the floor. A big red lampshade hung over the bed. The only thing in that whole room that wasn't red was the wall. It was black.

Stella stopped. She didn't look at me. "That's Mama's room," she said.

"Did your brother do all this too?"

"My brother hates it," Stella said. "Mama did it herself."

She moved down the hall and I reluctantly followed. We crossed the derelict sun porch and slammed the screen door on our way out.

I walked a full block with the vision of Stella's mama's room in my head. Alison was spared. She's been too well brought up to look in rooms she's not supposed to. Anyway, she could think of nothing but Stella's budget.

"Wouldn't it be more economical to shop at the super-market?" Alison asked her.

"It's economical anywhere I shop," Stella said. "Can't make nothing but grits and fried eggs. And peanut-butter sand-wiches."

"We get to take home economics next year," Alison said. "They teach you how to cook."

"That ought to make my brother happy," Stella said. "He's sure tired of peanut butter."

"Your mom's got a lot of cookbooks, Mary Frances," Alison suggested. "Why don't we take a look?"

When we arrived at my house, Stella and Alison cleared the cookbooks off the kitchen shelf. They pored over them while I got the glasses and Oreos out of the cupboard.

They began to get on my nerves, giggling over the recipes and discussing household finances. Stella claimed there was no dish in any of the cookbooks she could put together for a total outlay of fifty cents. "This dollar's got to last for two meals," she explained.

"If you shopped at the supermarket . . ." Alison began.

"You know even at the supermarket I couldn't stretch this fifty cents very far," Stella said. "Anyway, I kind of like Mrs. C.J."

We heard the front door slam. A moment later Pete raced into the kitchen, grinning to beat the band. He grabbed two Oreos from the box on the table. I poured him a glass of milk. He took it without looking at me and ran out of the room, spilling half of the milk on the floor.

I gazed at the spilled milk.

"Hey, Mary Frances," Stella cut in, "you know Pete goes to C.J.'s every day after school?"

"Does he?" I asked absently. I decided a dishcloth was just the thing to wipe up the milk and fetched it from the sink.

"Mrs. C.J. says he just sits there back of the cold case," Stella continued. "Don't do nothing. Just sits there."

"Well," I said, "Pete's kind of an independent kid."

"Mrs. C.J. says she's afraid of him," Stella went on. "She says he's very tough."

Alison laughed. "He certainly is. He must be the toughest six-year-old child in Monroe."

I threw the milk-soaked dishcloth into the sink. Alison and Stella sounded just like a couple of little old Monroe ladies. It seemed all they could talk about was cooking, shopping, and people's brothers.

I poured out the milk and tried to change the subject to something on a higher plane. I failed. Alison and Stella were hard at work discussing Miss Holloway's new boyfriend when Scrappy started barking.

"We've got company," I announced, hearing the gate squeak.

Alison and Stella took the hint and quieted down. A few moments later, Ronnie opened the screen door.

"Hey, Mary Frances," he said. "Stella, Alison. Sorry to interrupt the tea party."

"Come on in," I invited. "Could I interest you in a glass of milk?"

"Okay," he said. He leaned against the stove while I fetched another glass.

"Say," he said casually, "does your dad still have that old fishing rod, Mary Frances?"

"Of course," I said. "That's a family heirloom. It belonged to my grandfather."

"Think he'd lend it to me?" Ronnie asked.

"Well, I don't know." I carried the milk over to him. "You going fishing or something?"

"That was the general idea," he admitted. "George's dad just bought a small boat and we're taking it out on the lake tomorrow."

"Oh," I said. I thought fast. "Tell you what. I think Dad might lend you the fishing rod if I tell him you're going to teach me how to fish."

Ronnie put the milk down carefully. "Tomorrow?"

"Well, yes," I said. "Of course, if you know somebody else who has a fishing rod you can borrow . . ."

"Now you know I'd really like to take you along," Ronnie said, "but the lake's a long way out and you don't have a bike. You'd have to ride pillion on mine."

"I think I could manage it without falling off," I said dryly. "What time are we going?"

Ronnie gave in. "I'll come by at seven in the morning," he said. Then he grinned. "Just be sure you don't lean too far out of the boat. I don't want you to scare the fish. Thanks for the milk." He bounded out through the screen door and we heard him run through the gate.

Alison broke the silence.

"Really, Mary Frances," she said, "you haven't got any shame."

"I guess you're right," I admitted cheerfully.

"The boys I know," Stella added, "when they go fishing, they like to go alone. They never take girls along."

"Stella," I said, "I think Alison will back me up when I tell you that Ronnie doesn't know I'm a girl."

"That's true," Alison said. "Ronnie's very stupid about a lot of things," she added loyally.

I was thinking that the girls weren't so bad after all when Alison suddenly asked, "Are you going to make sandwiches?"

There it was again; all she could think about was cooking.

"Certainly not," I snapped. "We'll eat what we catch."

Alison laughed. "Mary Frances, you'd sure better eat a big breakfast."

"Y'all fishing for catfish?" Stella asked.

"Catfish and bass," I said. "That's all they have around here, isn't it, Alison?"

"I don't know," Alison replied. "I don't know anything about fishing."

"Now I don't know about bass," Stella said, "but you can't catch catfish without salt pork. Does your mama keep salt pork in the house?"

"I guess so," I said. "We eat a lot or it in beans and chili, stuff like that."

"You don't need a lot," Stella said. "Just a little speck, that'll do it. Those catfish, they love salt pork."

"How do you know so much about it, Stella?" I asked. "I thought none of the boys you know ever took girls fishing."

"My brother took me fishing once or twice," Stella explained. "After that, I'd just go out on my own. I didn't have a proper fishing rod, of course. Just a stick and a piece of string and a fishhook."

"And you caught catfish with that?" Alison asked, astonished.

"Nothing to it," Stella assured us. "Just need a little salt pork."

"Well, I don't know," I said. "I think the boys are going to use those artificial lures George is always talking about."

Stella laughed. "Alison's right," she said, and they grinned at each other. "You sure better eat a big breakfast, because you're sure not going to catch any lunch."

4

At a quarter to seven the next morning I was sitting on the curb outside my house, waiting for Ronnie. I didn't have long to wait. He rode up the street well before the appointed hour.

"Morning, Mary Frances," he said, leaning his bike against a tree. He picked up the fishing rod I was holding and balanced it in his palm. "That's a first-rate fishing rod," he remarked, handing it back. "Ready?"

"Sure," I said, picking up a paper sack I'd been sitting in front of.

"What's in the paper sack?" Ronnie asked immediately.

"Nothing much."

"Bait? We're not using bait. It's not sporting. We're using plugs. You know, artificial lures."

"Yes," I said. "Well, Stella insisted I take along this special kind of bait she recommended."

"Does Stella know how to fish?"

"She says she used to fish all the time."

"What did she fish for?"

"Catfish."

"We're not fishing for catfish," said Ronnie. "We're fishing for bass."

"I know."

"Of course, there are plenty of catfish in the lake, down near the bottom," Ronnie continued. "A lot of people go fishing for catfish out there." He paused. "I guess Stella would be insulted if we didn't take the bait along," he said finally.

"I guess so."

"That sure is a lot of bait."

"I guess so," I replied. "Shouldn't we go now?"

Ronnie shot me a piercing look. "If you don't tell me about it, Mary Frances, we're not going anywhere. There's something sinister going on."

"What gives you that idea?"

"You."

"Listen, if we don't go on, we'll miss all the fish."

"They're not going anywhere," Ronnie said. He regarded me a moment longer. "Okay. You just hop on the fender here in the back."

"Can't I ride on the handlebars?"

"You'll block my vision," he objected.

I climbed onto the fender, clutching the fishing rod and the paper sack in my right hand, and stuck my left arm around Ronnie's chest.

"Try not to fall off too often," he said, and we took off.

George's house is the only two-story house in Monroe. A long sweeping gravel drive cuts a path through the only lawn in Monroe that's soft and green, end to end, like a carpet. There are three tall marble pillars on the porch, holding up the house, I guess.

George was leaning against a pillar when we rode up across the lawn.

"Glad you could make it, Mary Frances," George said politely. "Hey, Ronnie. Ready?"

"We're just waiting for you," Ronnie said.

George started to hop onto his bike, propped up against another pillar, when he spotted the paper sack.

"What's in the sack?" he demanded.

"Stella's special bait," Ronnie explained.

"We're not using bait, Mary Frances."

"I know."

"I've got a lot of new plugs," George continued. "Made them myself. You'll see. They're first-rate. That sure looks like a lot of bait, Mary Frances."

"It's very bulky," I agreed.

Ronnie shot me another piercing look and then suddenly he laughed.

"Sandwiches!" he cried. "Your mom's made sandwiches."

"Not exactly," I said, embarrassed. "Fried chicken."

I was glad to see Ronnie was still smiling. "Your mom doesn't seem to think we're going to catch anything."

"Well, I guess not," I admitted. "She seemed to think I'll mess it up."

"You probably will," Ronnie agreed.

"That's not fair, Ronnie," George said, springing to my defense. "It's not Mary Frances' fault nobody ever showed her how to fish before. I'm sure she'll do just fine." He beamed at me.

I beamed back.

"Are you going to lead the convoy, George?" Ronnie cut in.

"Just a minute," George said. "Give me that fishing rod, Mary Frances."

I handed it over. He strapped it onto the basket, on top of his own fishing rod. Then he jumped on his bike and sped across the lawn, and we followed.

Florida is probably the soggiest state in the country. It's laced with rivers and streams and spotted with swampland. Miss Holloway says you can locate a town anywhere in Florida and still be no more than twenty miles away from a lake or river.

Monroe is no exception. The town lies about five miles south of an oval-shaped freshwater lake, half a mile long and a quarter of a mile wide. People probably drive by the lake every day and don't know it's there, because it's hidden behind a screen of live oak trees and strangler fig stumps.

The strangler figs are the result of a City Council project. A few years ago, the City Council decided to spruce up the lake. They planted strangler figs around the shore and among the live oaks. Those trees never took hold. They died off, one by one, leaving brittle dried-out stumps. About the only things that grow around the lake now are the live oaks and cattails.

The City Council also built a pier out into the lake, just at the end of a narrow winding path from the road through the trees. That part of the Monroe public who can afford boats keeps them out in the open, tied up to the pier. A giant live oak shelters the pier from the worst of the wind and the rain.

I spotted George's boat as soon as we rounded the last curve in the path. It was the only one of the seven boats floating on the lake with a tarpaulin stretched across it. I jumped off Ronnie's bike and stood out of the way, clutching my paper sack.

George leaned his bike against a tree, unstrapped the fishing rods, picked up a green metal bait box from the basket on his bike, and jogged to the boat. Ronnie followed George. I followed Ronnie.

"Hold on to these, Mary Frances," George said, handing me the fishing rods and the bait box. While Ronnie and George peeled back the tarpaulin, I sat on the pier and opened the bait box.

I closed the lid quickly and looked around. Ronnie was grinning at me. I opened the lid again.

They were not shrunken heads, I was relieved to see. Nor were they caterpillars. I peered closely at one object and recognized some of my own hair, braided, twisted, and tied with a bit of string. It looked like a worm wearing a grass skirt. Next to it was an object that looked like a shaggy red mouse. I suddenly realized that it was made out of George's hair.

Close examination revealed a fish made out of Alison's hair, two frogs fashioned from Ronnie's hair, and a six-legged spider made from the hair of Bobby Stone. That had to be Bobby's hair, because it was snow white. Bobby's had white hair since I can remember.

"This must have taken you months, George," I said as Ronnie tucked the tarpaulin under a seat in the boat.

"I worked on them all summer," George boomed. He jogged over. "Remember when I asked you for a lock of your hair? That's it, over there. The worm."

"I thought it looked familiar."

"Bass go for these bugs," George explained. "The Seminoles have always used them up along the creeks. They make them out of deer hair. I figured our hair would do just as good. Touch it," he said.

I did. "That's pretty stiff!"

"Dipped them in paraffin," George explained. "Keeps out the water. Otherwise, one or two casts and they're water logged."

"That's great, George," I said. "Where are the hooks?"

"Look into this spray here at the end," George said. He parted the spray at the end of the curly fish. The hook stuck out of that.

"Now, under this shelf here, we've got the poppers," George went on. He lifted out the top half of the box.

The poppers weren't half so interesting. They looked like little metal disks pressed down in the middle, with hooks hanging off the end.

"I don't know," I said doubtfully. "Think they'll work?"

"We'll find out," George said. "Bought them down on Lee. The man said they pop when they hit the water, and the bass think they're some kind of bug and come on over to look."

"They don't look like bugs," I pointed out.

"I'm not sure the fish can tell the difference," George said.

"I suppose we're going to catch enough bass with these things to last all winter," I said optimistically.

"I wouldn't be surprised," George said. "Better get started."

I sprang to my feet, overturning the bait box. The hair lures spilled out onto the pier.

"Oh, George," I said, stricken. "I'll pick them up. Ouch. Ouch. Wow. Ouch."

This painful incident taught me more than I wanted to know about hair lures. I think I found every hook in every bug. Half my fingers were bleeding by the time we got the lures back in the box.

"Just stick your hand in the water, Mary Frances," George advised me. "That'll stop the bleeding."

George always gives first-rate medical advice. That isn't surprising, because his dad is a doctor. George always knows what works for cuts and bruises and broken fingers, even if he doesn't quite know why it works. We all follow his advice faithfully.

I leaned over the edge of the dock and stuck my hands in the water.

"That's not the way to catch fish, Mary Frances," Ronnie yelled from the boat.

"Don't be funny," I growled.

George was right; the shock of the cold water stopped the bleeding. I walked casually to the boat as if nothing had happened.

George had laid our gear on the bottom of the boat, under the seats. He whipped me up and swung me into the boat. Then he leaped in after me.

50

"Sit down, Mary Frances," Ronnie said. "You're going to capsize the boat."

"I know how to balance myself in a boat," I said. I sat down carefully. George started the engine and we were off.

We dropped anchor in the middle of the lake. Each of the boys took a fishing rod. I was in charge of supplies. In practical terms, that meant I got to fill a large plastic bucket with lake water and sit watching the boys fish.

Ronnie cast out his line and reeled it in empty for half an hour before he remembered he was supposed to be teaching me how to fish.

"Just watch me, Mary Frances," he said. "When you cast out, you keep your thumb hovering over the reel here, so you can keep the line straight and stop it when you want to."

He demonstrated.

"When the plug hits the water, you stop it like this."

He demonstrated.

"Now, bass swim near the top of the water. You let that plug sink to the bottom, and you might get a catfish. We're not looking for catfish. We're fishing for bass."

"Your plug just sank to the bottom," I said helpfully.

Ronnie scowled at me. He reeled in his line and cast it out again.

"I'm using a popper," Ronnie said. "If you get any plug hopping, the bass are going to think it's a real bug. So you jerk it—short little jerks like that."

I nodded my head.

"If a fish bites, you'll feel a tug, and then you reel your line in slowly, like this."

He demonstrated.

"Not all at once," he cautioned. "Sometimes you want to let the fish run with it."

"I understand," I said, reaching for the fishing rod. Ronnie didn't seem to notice. He cast out his line.

The boys continued for another half hour. George was using hair lures. Ronnie stuck to the poppers.

Nothing happened.

I sat patiently, watching them cast out, reel in, and cast out again.

George switched to the poppers.

Nothing happened.

"I don't understand," George said. "These plugs ought to work."

"May I try?" I asked.

"Mary Frances," Ronnie said, "if we can't get a bite, you'll never be able to catch anything. At least we know what we're doing. They're just not biting today."

"I don't know," George said. "Mary Frances might be lucky." He beamed at me. I beamed back. It occurred to me that I had never appreciated George as much as I appreciated him at that moment.

"Why don't you let me tie on the plugs, at least?" I offered.

"Okay, Mary Frances," George said. "It might bring us luck."

"She can tie on your plug if she likes," Ronnie said, "but I think I'll do my own. The way she ties knots, we'll lose all these plugs at the bottom of the lake."

That did it. I made up my mind.

George handed me his fishing rod.

"Go ahead and cast," I said. "I want to choose a plug."

The minute his back was turned, I reached into the paper sack, picked a tiny piece of bait, and hid it in the palm of my hand.

Turning to the bait box, I chose the red shaggy mouse. I figured I'd been stuck by enough of the hooks to know where they were without stabbing myself. Keeping my eyes on the boys, I carefully worked a speck of salt pork onto the hook and pushed it into the spray of red hair.

George was just reeling in when I'd finished.

"No luck," he said. "Mary Frances, why don't you try it?"

"Oh, no," I said. "I just love watching you boys fish. I'll just tie on this fine bug."

George handed me the fishing rod. I cut off the popper and tied on the shaggy mouse.

"Let me see the knot," Ronnie said.

I believe my heart stopped a moment. Ronnie couldn't fail to notice the bait, however well I'd hidden it.

"I'm sure it's all right," George said. He took the rod and cast out the line without hesitating.

Thirty seconds after the lure hit the water, the line grew taut.

"Hey, George, you got a fish!" I yelled.

"I know," George boomed. I'd never seen him so excited. "Two-pound bass or I'm mistaken," he added, and reeled in slowly. "Get the bucket ready, Mary Frances!" he shouted.

I held the bucket right next to George's elbow. He leaned out over the water and grabbed the end of his line, dropped the wriggling fish into the bucket, and carefully disengaged the hook. We all gazed respectfully at the fish, gliding around in the bucket.

"That's a fine bass," Ronnie said. "Half a pound at least."

George beamed. "Half a pound or I'm mistaken," he boomed, and cast out his line again before I could stop him.

The line grew taut a few seconds after the lure hit the water, and a flat blue panfish joined the bass in the bucket. It occurred to me that maybe George didn't need Stella's bait after all.

Or maybe he did. Fifteen more minutes of casting out and reeling in produced no visible results. George handed me his fishing rod.

"This rod works a little differently from your dad's, Mary Frances," George explained. "It's a newer model." He demonstrated the buttons and levers on the reel. "It's pretty easy, once you get the hang of it. Why don't you give it a try?"

I was ready. I cut off the mouse and tied on a shaggy frog lure I'd loaded with a tiny speck of bait. I cast out.

Nothing happened. I was beginning to reel in slowly when I felt a tug and the line grew taut.

"George!" I yelled. "What do I do now?"

"Just hold on, Mary Frances," George said. "Now reel in real slow. That's it, real slow. That does it. There."

George leaned out over the edge of the boat and grabbed my line.

"That's a fine catfish, Mary Frances," he said, dropped it into the bucket and disengaged the hook.

"Except we're fishing for bass," Ronnie mumbled.

"Better than nothing," I said philosophically. I regarded my fish critically. "Do you think it's over the weight limit?"

Ronnie couldn't resist an intellectual problem like this one. He leaned over to look into the bucket.

"Just over the limit, Mary Frances," he said. "That's a full-grown catfish, all right. Just a little undersized." He grinned. "I guess a shrimp like you would have to catch a shrimp like that."

"I believe you're jealous," I remarked.

Ronnie laughed and returned to his fruitless casting. I handed the fishing rod back to George.

"You can use it again, Mary Frances," George said. "You should never stop when you're getting lucky."

"I don't know," I said. "I think I'll quit while I'm ahead."

George cast out. I loaded a curly fish bug with a scrap of bait. I was ready for George when he handed me the rod.

"Could you tie on another plug, Mary Frances?" he asked. "You seem to bring me luck."

That was the way it went until hunger drove us off the

lake. If George caught a fish with a loaded lure, he caught another fish soon afterward, when the lure was empty. He'd go on trying for twenty minutes or half an hour without any luck, and then he'd hand me his fishing rod, and I'd tie on a newly loaded lure. It seems all he needed was a little luck—and a bit of bait now and again.

Around noon, Ronnie tied a popper on to his line and managed to land a bass. I tried my hand again and caught another undersized catfish. Ronnie said I was letting my plug sink too far. I ignored him.

We called it a day about one o'clock, pulled up anchor, and chugged back to the pier.

George leaped onto the pier and I handed him the fishing rods and the bait box. Then George swung me up onto the pier.

"I'll stow these on my bike," he said, picking up the gear and jogging into the trees.

Ronnie was crouched in the boat, fiddling with the tarpaulin.

"Hey, Ronnie," I called. "How many fish did we catch?"

Ronnie peered into the bucket. "Hard to tell," he said. "They're having a relay race in there." He studied the bucket. "Two bass, four panfish, and two shrimps."

"That's two bass, four panfish, and two catfish," I corrected him.

"Oh, no," Ronnie said. "I know a shrimp when I see one. Those are definitely shrimps. Take a look for yourself."

I leaned out over the edge of the pier to grab the bucket.

I guess I heard George jogging back up the pier, but I didn't think anything of it until I felt a thump and found myself flying through the air. I grabbed instinctively for anything I could hold. Unfortunately, what I grabbed was the fish bucket, and I took it with me as I plunged into the lake.

The sight that greeted me when I came up for air wasn't worth falling into the lake for, but it made me laugh just the same. George and Ronnie were staring at the spot where I'd gone under. I'd never seen two such stricken faces in my life. I thought they were going to cry.

Ronnie dispelled any notion I may have had that his sorrow was on my account. "The bucket, Mary Frances!" he yelled, spotting me. "The bucket! Get the bucket!"

I ignored him.

"It's my fault, Mary Frances," George boomed. "I didn't see you."

"Could you just give me a hand, George?" I asked as calmly as I could. "This lake water's pretty cold for swimming."

George pulled me out onto the pier. I stood there dripping.

"I don't know why, I just didn't see you," George said, unbuttoning his shirt.

"That's okay, George."

"Take off your shirt, Mary Frances."

"George!" I said, shocked. It seemed Ronnie wasn't the only person who didn't know I was a girl.

George's face suddenly turned as red as his hair. "You can go over behind that tree and put this on," he said, handing me his shirt. "Dad says it's not healthy to stand around in wet clothes."

I decided George knew what he was talking about. I took his shirt and disappeared behind a live oak tree.

The boys had stretched the tarpaulin over the boat by the time I emerged, wringing out my shirt and cut-offs. Ronnie was standing on the dock, holding the pail. His expression was tragic.

He seemed to cheer up when he saw me. In fact, he laughed.

"Where did you get that shirt, Mary Frances?"

"It's George's shirt."

"It comes down to your ankles."

"I know it comes down to my ankles. George is six feet tall." I spread my clothes out on the pier to dry in the sun.

"Hey, Mary Frances," Ronnie yelled.

I turned around and Ronnie threw me the bucket. He threw it high and wide, and I missed it. It bounced on the pier.

"Oh," I said.

"They got away," Ronnie said. "Every last fish swam out of that bucket back into the lake. A whole morning wasted."

"We've still got Mrs. Allen's fried chicken," George said, jogging up the pier with my paper sack.

We sat on the pier and shared it out. By the time we'd finished it, my clothes were dry and I ducked back behind the live oak to change back into them. When I returned, Ronnie was peering into the paper sack.

"What's all this salt pork for, Mary Frances?" he asked.

"That's Stella's special bait," I explained. "She says catfish love salt pork. She thought bass might like it too."

"Are you serious?" George asked. "I never heard of that. Salt pork?"

"Well," I said, "it's probably one of those old backcountry legends. I guess your plugs are about the best in the world for catching bass."

George smiled at me. "They seemed to do all right," he said.

"Too bad Mary Frances destroyed the evidence," Ronnie said.

"It was your idea," I reminded him. "You were handing me the bucket. Anyway," I went on in a conciliatory fashion, "it's not whether you win or lose, it's how you play the game."

"Huh?" said George.

"We took the boat out," I explained, "and we got in a lot of good fishing."

"That's true," George said. "You know, Mary Frances, you brought us luck. I think you can come again with us, anytime."

"Not on your life," Ronnie growled.

"It's not your boat," I reminded Ronnie haughtily. I turned to George. "Whenever you boys like," I said, and smiled.

George and I were beaming at one another when Ronnie grabbed my arm and pulled me off to his bike. "It's a long way back to town," he said. "Hop on. Try not to fall off. Here, take this." He handed me Dad's fishing rod.

Ronnie was silent all the way back to town. We were just pulling into my street when he spoke up.

"I guess those plugs of George's are pretty good," he said.

"They look real nice," I agreed.

Ronnie stopped the bike and I jumped off.

"Thanks for the ride," I said, and turned toward the house.

"Mary Frances," Ronnie said suddenly.

I whirled around.

"Mary Frances," Ronnie said. "You didn't do anything to those lures, did you? When you tied on those lures?"

"Certainly not," I said heatedly. "George caught those fish without any help from anybody. Of course, I probably brought him luck."

Ronnie looked at me long and hard. Then he laughed. "One of you girls did, anyway," he said, and rode off.

5

Miss Holloway announced the mapmaking competition just before Thanksgiving.

"The best way to learn about a country," she said, "is to make a map of it."

A couple of people groaned.

"There will be a prize for the best map," Miss Holloway went on, pretending she hadn't heard.

Stella stuck up her hand.

"What kind of prize, ma'am?" she asked.

"I haven't decided."

Ronnie stuck his hand up. "I think a fishing rod would be a good prize," he suggested.

"You haven't won yet," said Miss Holloway. "We'll see about the prize. Now I want you to form teams, with two people to each team. Let me have the names this afternoon. I'll want the maps turned in next week."

I caught up with Stella in the lunchroom.

"Would you like to team up with me?" I asked, setting my tray down next to hers.

Stella looked surprised. "Aren't you going to team up with Alison?"

"Why should I team up with Alison?"

"Well, she's your best friend and all."

"We don't let emotion interfere with business," I explained, and took a bite out of my hamburger.

Stella didn't consider that a very good explanation. "What are you talking about?"

"Alison's got to make good grades."

"Why?"

"Because her parents want her to," I said. "They're very strict. They make her study all the time. They have big plans for her."

"What kind of plans?"

"Well, they want her to go to college, for one thing," I said. "Anyway, she can't afford to take chances, because they make her life real miserable if she doesn't bring home good grades."

"What do they do?"

"It's hard to explain." I cast around for an example. "I remember one time when we were small, Alison brought home a C in math. She had A's in everything else. Her mother didn't even look at the A's. She just looked at that C, and then she looked at Alison with a sad, pitiful expression, and she said, 'Well, Alison, if that's the best you can do, we'll have to accept it. Your father and I are very disappointed in you.' It made me feel cold all over just hearing it. Alison's never brought home a C since."

Stella was silent for a bit, and I finished my hamburger. Then she asked suddenly, "What's that got to do with the map contest?"

"Whenever there's a contest," I explained, "Alison always teams up with Ronnie. They're the two smartest kids in school and they always win."

"Oh," Stella said. She thought a moment. "I thought Ronnie would team up with George. George is his faithful sidekick."

"His what?"

"Faithful sidekick."

"What's that?"

"His friend," Stella said. "That's what my papa used to call it."

"That's pretty good," I said. "Ronnie doesn't team up with his faithful sidekick because his faithful sidekick is as dumb as I am. Ronnie wants to make good grades too."

"I guess his parents make him, too."

"His parents can't make him do anything. Ronnie does what he likes. What he likes to do is make good grades. He's very ambitious."

"You sure got a lot of ambitious friends," Stella remarked.

"Oh, I don't know," I said. "I'm not ambitious. And George isn't ambitious. Of course, he doesn't have to be."

"Why not?"

"Because George's grandfather was a judge, and his dad is a doctor, and George will get into college and later he'll get into law school whether he makes good grades or not. Now take Ronnie, he's got five little brothers. You know it takes a lot of money to raise a family that big, and there's nothing left over for college or anything. Ronnie's got to do it by himself. Look, do you want to team up with me or not?"

"Okay," Stella said. "I'm not real ambitious either."

We got our assignments that afternoon.

"I think it will be more democratic if we assign countries alphabetically," Miss Holloway said. My heart sank. "Mary Frances," she went on, "you and Stella will make a map of Afghanistan."

"Afghanistan?" I said, horrified. "Where's that?"

"Asia," Miss Holloway said. She calmly continued the list, assigning countries like Great Britain and Greece and Peru. Every team drew an easy country, with the notable exception of mine.

I apologized to Stella after school.

"That's okay," Stella said. "Maybe it's interesting."

We strolled over to the public library to look Afghanistan up in the encyclopedia. Expecting the worst, I asked Stella to read the entry and tell me what she found.

"Well, just look at that," she said, studying the encyclopedia. "It's got mountains, deserts, and camels."

That didn't cheer me up. "Can you draw a camel?"

"Hey, wait a minute," Stella said. "What are we supposed to make this map out of?"

"That's a good question," I said. "I don't know. What do you think?"

"Miss Holloway didn't say."

"Maybe we're supposed to buy cardboard and paints and glue," I suggested.

Stella looked depressed.

I knew it was hopeless to offer to pay for the supplies myself. Stella would insist on paying half.

"What if you don't buy any orange sodas."

"We got one week," Stella said. "My brother gives me a dime a day for myself."

We walked slowly out of the library. Stella was deep in thought.

We had nearly reached Second Street when she spoke.

"Hey," she said. "What about rocks and grass and dirt?"

"What about it?" I said, puzzled.

"I'll show you. Come on."

I had no idea where we were going, but I followed Stella anyway, up Second Street. She disappeared into the vacant lot.

We climbed over the great roots of banyan trees and ducked under the Spanish moss hanging thick from every tree, great and small. A couple of times a stray branch hit me in the face. I guess a lot of Florida used to look like this. Now there's just the vacant lot, an isolated piece of tangled wilderness.

"I used to play here when I was a kid," I said when we reached the first clearing.

"Look," Stella said. She picked up a rock. "This can be a mountain. Look at all this grass." She broke off a twig. "This can be a tree."

I finally caught on. "All we have to buy is cardboard and paste," I said.

"Not even," Stella said. "I guess Mrs. C.J. would give us an old cardboard box."

We went straight to the public library after school the next afternoon. Stella brought along a big piece of cardboard. I brought the paste I'd bought for a dime at the supermarket.

"We don't need that yet," Stella said. "Anyway, here's my nickel," she added, sliding it across the table. "Got a pencil?"

I handed it over.

"What we got to do is trace a map."

"We can't trace anything on cardboard," I pointed out. "It's too thick. I don't suppose Mrs. C.J. has any tracing paper."

"Not to give away."

Stella studied the map in the encyclopedia. "Don't matter," she said finally. "Look how little it is. I guess we'll have to do it freehand."

To my surprise, Stella had a very sure hand. In no time at all, she'd reproduced the outlines of Afghanistan four times the size of the map in the encyclopedia.

"Boy, you're really good," I said. "Where did you learn to draw?"

"I didn't," Stella said. "Never had anything to draw with before."

We both studied the encyclopedia in silence.

"Okay," Stella said. "Mountains . . . they got mountains here, in the middle."

We spent the rest of the afternoon marking mountains, valleys, deserts, grasslands, rivers, and things like that.

On Saturday morning, we went out into the field, as Ronnie might say. We crashed through the vacant lot, map and paste in hand, and settled in the clearing.

"I guess maybe we ought to start with the deserts," Stella said.

We slopped a bit of paste on the cardboard, and then we gathered up dirt and pressed it down.

"Pretty good," Stella said when we'd finished. "Now we got to break up grass."

"Why do we have to break it up?"

"We're showing grasslands," Stella said. "This size of this grass on a bitty map like this, it'll look like a jungle."

I had to admit she was right. We broke up a few blades of grass and scattered them loosely over the corner of the map, to see how they looked.

"Not bad," I said. "Wait a minute, I'll get the paste open."

I reached for the paste pot, disturbing a green snake that had wound itself around it.

"Hey," I said. "Get off that paste."

The snake slid off, straight onto the map. It hunched up its back and inched its way across.

"Just look at that," Stella said, grinning. The snake inched its way through the grasslands, displacing blades of grass on its winding way. It slid off the map, climbed over Stella's leg and disappeared into the bushes.

"I guess we got a river," Stella said. She marked the snake's trail. "Anyway," she added, "it's close enough to where the river really is. Just a little more winding."

"More artistic," I agreed.

"I sure wish I had a pet," Stella said as we pasted the grass into place.

"Like a snake?"

"Well," Stella said. "These little green snakes, they're all right. They don't hurt nobody. But they like to be free. And there's all kinds of snakes. There's water moccasins. You ever see a water moccasin?"

"I'm glad to say I haven't."

"I saw one once," Stella said. "We were living near the Everglades. It bit some little kid right on the thigh. Nasty-looking things, them old water moccasins. Seemed to come up right out of the canal."

"What happened?"

"The kid started screaming and then he collapsed."

"Did he die?"

"Well, I called my brother and he came and lanced the wound with his penknife and sucked out the venom."

"That's wonderful!" I said.

"He saw a movie once," Stella said. "The little kid was sick for a while but he recovered."

"I bet your brother is amazing!"

"Yeah."

We worked on in silence.

"I had a pet once," Stella said suddenly.

"What kind of a pet?"

"A chicken," she answered. "I wish you could have seen that chicken. I called her Rosie. She was just like a dog. I could say, 'Here, Rosie,' and Rosie would come running. She could even do tricks. I could say, 'Dance, Rosie,' and whistle a tune, and Rosie danced. Mama said I was stupid, making a pet out of a chicken. Anyway, Rosie's dead now."

"I guess chickens don't live very long," I said comfortingly.

"Rosie would've lived a lot longer if my uncle had stayed in Atlanta," Stella said angrily.

"Oh," I said. "Did he kill her?"

"In a way," Stella said. "Mama really admires my uncle. He's a rich man, she says, owns a used-car lot in Atlanta. He came to visit one day, my uncle and aunt and four kids.

"You know what we used to eat in those days?" Stella went on. "Once, twice a month we got hamburgers. Most days it was grits and greens and a little salt pork, and catfish when me or my brother caught any. It was good enough for us. But it wasn't good enough for my uncle. The day my uncle arrived, Mama sent me off to school. When I got home, I couldn't find Rosie. I asked everybody if they'd seen her and everybody said, 'Forget about Rosie. It's just a stupid chicken.'

"Mama sent me out back to wash for dinner and comb my hair and put on my good clothes." Stella grinned. "I didn't have no good clothes. Then we were all sitting around the table and Mama went to the stove and brought out Rosie."

I was horrified. "Are you sure it was Rosie?"

"Don't you think I'd know my own chicken," Stella said, "even plucked and dead like that? It was Rosie."

"What did you do?"

"I told my uncle and aunt and four cousins they were eating Rosie for dinner," Stella said. "Mama was so furious she sent me away from the table. I couldn't have eaten Rosie anyway. I ran away from home."

"Where did you go?"

"Couldn't go very far," she said. "There was just the swamp. Man"—she grinned again—"the mosquitoes were terrible. My brother came and got me the next day."

"Look," I said, "you could have a dog. Nobody's going to eat a dog."

"I'm not so sure," Stella said. "My uncle comes to town, Mama, she'd cook anything. There," she said, holding up the map. "Desert and grasslands and a river, all pasted on firm. Got to go home." She stuck the cardboard map under her arm and crashed out of the lot.

I recounted the story of Stella's chicken to my rapt family at dinner that night. When I had finished, Dad looked at Mom. To my surprise, Mom began to protest.

"It's not the same thing," she said.

"What's not the same thing?" I asked.

Nobody paid any attention to me.

"What is the difference between Mrs. Shanks's blood sacrifice," Dad asked, "and your budget sacrifice?"

"It's two different worlds," Mom said.

"I fail to see the difference," Dad said. "It costs us a week's food money every time your brother, the county prosecutor, comes to dinner."

"That's entirely different!"

"In what way?"

"Well," Mom said, and couldn't think of one.

"Now don't misunderstand me," Dad said. "I like tunafish casserole."

I'll say he did. Dad had had three helpings already.

"But why don't you serve it when your brother comes to call?" Dad asked. "I suppose only T-bone steaks and loin lamb chops are good enough for a gentleman in his elevated position. And look at the children."

Mom looked at us.

"At the moment," Dad said, "they look like ragpickers. But when your sainted brother is a guest in our home, little Pete looks like the crown prince of all the Russias and Mary Frances looks like a film star. Isn't that your doing?"

Mom had to admit it was.

"We're going to have to straighten out our values in this family," Dad said, fixing each of us in turn with a very steely eye.

"That poor woman," Mom said quietly. I wasn't sure whether she was talking about Stella's mother or herself.

6

On Monday afternoon, Stella and I headed for the vacant lot to gather mountains for our map. We found several small pebbles and one splendid sharp rock, craggy enough to serve as a whole mountain range by itself.

I was just opening the paste pot when we heard somebody crashing through the lot. We waited, and presently Alison emerged from the brush.

"I thought I'd find you here," she said in greeting.

"How did you know?" I asked.

"Ronnie spotted you," she said. "We're on our way to the supermarket for pastels."

"What's a pastel?" Stella asked.

"Chalk," Alison said. "England has a gentle landscape, all rolling hills and dales, so we're doing our map in pastels. They're soft and gentle colors. We've run out of dark green. Listen," she went on, "you won't believe what that stupid C.J.'s done now."

"Try us," I said.

"He's got a dead rat," Alison said. "He's holding it up by the tail. . . . Hey, where are you going?"

I raced out of the vacant lot and ran across the street. Sure enough, there was C.J., standing halfway between the gas pump and the door. He was swinging Pete's mouse by the tail.

"What did you do that for?" I yelled at him.

C.J. was pretty proud of himself. "Mashed in its head with a hammer," he said. "Bet you didn't know we had a mouse."

Stella and Alison raced up, out of breath. "Hey, what's the matter?" Stella asked.

"You better get rid of that mouse," I warned C.J.

"Trouble with you kids today, you got no respect," C.J. growled. "Watch your mouth."

Ronnie sauntered out of the store, drinking a Nehi. "What's the excitement?"

"Look at that mouse," I said. "He's murdered it."

C.J. lost his temper. "You kids git outa here," he yelled. "You're trespassing on private property. Go on, git."

"Why did you kill the mouse?" Ronnie asked, in a reasonable tone.

Now C.J. might consider Stella a dumb kid, Alison an uppity black and me a pudgy part of the landscape. But even C.J. know how smart Ronnie is. He deigned to answer.

"I got a right to kill anything I want on my property," C.J. said. "This is my store. See that gas pump? That's mine. Everything you see belongs to me." He swung the mouse toward the door, where Emily and Mrs. C.J. were standing, watching us. "My wife and my little girl, they belong to me. Far as you can see, everything is my property."

"Not that mouse," I said. "That's Pete's mouse. Pete sees that, he'll die. He'll kill you."

"Always thought there was something wrong with that crazy kid," C.J. said.

"You watch your mouth," I said. "You watch what you say about my brother."

Nobody noticed Pete until he struck. Suddenly there he was, pounding on C.J.'s fat belly, kicking the fat man in the knee. I guess the element of surprise accounted for Pete's success, because C.J. dropped the mouse at once. Pete scooped it up and

70

ran across the street into the vacant lot, leaving C.J. open-mouthed, gasping for air.

I raced after Pete. I found him in the clearing, cradling the mouse.

"It's dead," I said. "C.J. killed it."

"I'll kill him," Pete said.

"I guess you will," I said. "What are you going to do with the mouse?"

Pete mumbled something.

"What's that?" I asked.

Pete favored me with his customary glare. We sat there in silence until we heard people crashing through the lot.

Stella was the first to arrive. "Gonna bury it?"

Pete nodded.

"Where?" she asked.

"Here, I guess," Ronnie said, crashing through. He was followed closely by Alison.

"Can't," Pete said. "Snakes."

"A little snake isn't going to bother with a mouse," I said.

"That depends," Stella said. "Now some snakes, like the python, they'll eat anything. Elephants. You never know."

"Chickens," Pete said.

"Yeah," Stella agreed. "Even chickens."

Pete was gazing at Stella with a strange, surprised expression. I suddenly realized that, even though Pete never said much, he listened all the time. He was looking at Stella and thinking of Rosie. I guess it's the first time he'd ever shared anything with anybody. Stella had mourned a pet, too.

"The lot's out," Stella said. "It's not safe."

We sat around thinking.

"You don't have any snakes at your house," Alison said.

"Hey, that's a good idea," Stella said. "Bury it in your yard."

"Right," Pete said. We all walked slowly to the house.

Alison and I rummaged through my dresser and came up with a suitable box. Stella sent us back to get a handful of Kleenex to line it with. Ronnie fetched a spade and we started through the gate.

Scrappy started to bark.

"Wait a minute," Stella said. "We can't bury him in the backyard."

"Why not?" I said.

Stella whispered to me. "Dogs, you know, they dig things up."

"Right," I announced. "We're going to bury him here in the front yard."

And so we did, right outside my bedroom window. Ronnie patted the mound smooth, Alison picked a hibiscus blossom and laid it on the top, and Stella put two sticks together for a cross. She stuck it at the head of the mound. Pete mumbled something.

"What'd you say?" Stella asked him.

Pete didn't glare at Stella, the way he usually glared at me. He just spoke up so that she could hear.

"What if a mouse ain't a Baptist," Pete said loudly.

"Other people get crosses," Stella said. "You have to be a Christian, is all."

"What if a mouse ain't a Christian," Pete said stubbornly. "What if he's something else."

"Could be," Stella said. We all stood around wondering what to say. "I'll ask my brother," Stella said finally. "Anyway, I guess a cross will do as good as anything. He's got to have something."

Pete looked at the little mound and then ran through the gate into the backyard.

We stood there helpless, looking at one another, and then Ronnie said quietly, "Mary Frances, C.J. can't keep getting away with it."

"He's just ignorant, is all," Stella said.

"That's no excuse," Alison said. "It's bad enough, the way he insults people. It's bad enough, the way he treats his poor family. But when he starts picking on a little kid like Pete, he's gone too far."

"He didn't know that was Pete's mouse," Stella pointed out. "He's just an ignorant old drunken man. Look, I better get back there and get the map. I left it on C.J.'s bench."

"Stella's right, Alison," Ronnie said. "C.J.'s not worth the trouble."

"Ronnie Bean!" Alison said, shocked. "You don't mean to say you approve of that old man."

"I wouldn't say that," Ronnie said. "I stand corrected. He's not worth the trouble today, that's all. Come on. We'd better get to the supermarket before it closes."

I watched them leave, and then I looked over the gate. Pete was lying across Doggo, his head buried in the old dog's furry neck. I decided it would be a good idea to leave him alone.

Dad arrived for dinner at six, very perplexed.

"Have you children been performing religious rites on our expensive lawn?" he asked me. "I don't know that I care for the practice of displaying religious symbols. Seems a bit show-offy."

Before I could explain, he noticed that Pete's chair was empty. "Where's your brother?"

"He's out in the backyard," I said. "I don't think he's very hungry."

"What's he doing out there?" Mom wanted to know.

I told them. Mom and Dad looked at each other. Then Dad rose from the table and headed toward the kitchen. I heard the kitchen door open and shut.

Mom and I sat silently until Dad returned, his expression grave and troubled.

"I've excused Pete from dinner," Dad said, and picked up

his napkin. "You might leave a plate for him in the kitchen, Margaret. He might get hungry later on."

I looked into the backyard just before I went to bed. Pete was curled up next to Doggo, his arm thrown across the dog's back, and both were asleep. Sombody had covered them with a blanket.

Stella must have finished our map herself, because she handed it in the next day. The rocks looked very dramatic marching across the middle of the map.

There was a full-scale dress rehearsal after school for the Thanksgiving pageant. It went pretty well, I thought, as well as it should have. Monroe School is very proud of its traditions. In practical terms, that means that every Thanksgiving pageant is exactly the same, year after year. At this dress rehearsal, as at all Thanksgiving pageant dress rehearsals in the past, the choir sang "Bless This House," the actors ran through the annual skit, and the band played "America the Beautiful," followed by "Dixie."

The dress rehearsal lasted so long that I just had time to feed the dogs before sliding into my chair at the dinner table. I noticed Pete was in his seat.

Halfway through dinner, he spoke. "Dad," he said.

Now this was unusual, but not extraordinary. Dad, Mom and I turned to Pete, wondering whether he wanted the butter, the bread, or the peas.

"Yes, Pete," Dad responded.

"I want . . ." He stopped. We waited. He started again, speaking very carefully. "I want to invite Stella and Billy to Thanksgiving."

One advantage to never saying very much is that people really listen when you do speak up. However, they don't always give satisfactory answers.

"I believe that's your mother's department," Dad said.

Mom rose to the occasion. "Of course," she said. "But Thanksgiving's just two days away. They probably have other plans."

"Nope," Pete said. "I asked Billy."

I couldn't stand it any longer. "Who's Billy?"

Pete ignored me.

"Who's Billy?" Mom asked.

"Billy," Pete said, disgusted at our ignorance. "Billy!"

"That's all very well," Dad said, "but if your mother is going to invite him she'll have to know where to find him."

"Stella's house," Pete said.

It struck us all at the same time.

"Billy's Stella's brother," I said.

Pete did not bother to confirm my clever deduction.

"Well," Mom said, "we ought to invite Mrs. Shanks as well. I'll go by early tomorrow morning."

I got the sinking feeling that Mom wasn't going to get past the front porch. She's not a snob, but she's had a sheltered life. She really believes that everybody lives in a three-bedroom ranch house with stucco walls and a real fireplace.

"Listen, Mom," I said, "appearances are deceiving."

"What does that mean?" Dad asked.

"The place looks like a dump," I explained, "but inside it's real nice. Don't judge by the sun porch."

"I think you can trust me to behave properly," Mom said, insulted.

"Sorry," I said. Sometimes I think Pete has the right idea. There isn't much danger of saying the wrong thing if you never say anything at all.

The next morning I went straight to the auditorium and slipped into my choir robe. The pageant was scheduled for nine o'clock.

It rattled along on schedule. The principal opened the festivities with a speech. He told us all about the meaning of Thanksgiving. He said Thanksgiving means that we should all give thanks that we live in America, particularly in Monroe, where we all have enough food to eat and it never gets very cold in the winter.

The choir swung into "Bless This House." The altos remembered their parts.

There was a weird skit about Pilgrims.

The band played "America the Beautiful," and the audience filed out to the rousing rhythm of "Dixie."

I caught up with Stella in the lunchroom line and told her that Mom was inviting her family for dinner the next day.

Stella's reaction struck me as a bit odd.

"My whole family?"

"I believe so."

"My mama too?" Stella persisted.

"Well, yeah, I think," I said.

"Lord," Stella said. "I hope Mama doesn't laugh."

"Why should your mama laugh at being invited to a Thanksgiving dinner?"

"She's got a funny sense of humor," Stella said, and refused to explain any further.

7

I am not allowed into Mom's kitchen when serious work is in progress. This is because I have a tendency to break things, or spill things, or pour sugar on the steaks under the impression that I am salting them. So I was lounging around in the backyard at two o'clock the next day when Stella came through the gate.

"Hey," I said. "You're early. Dinner's not till four."

"I know that," Stella said. "Thought I'd come over early and see if I could help."

"I don't know," I said. "Mom doesn't like people under her feet much."

Stella looked disappointed. "I thought maybe I could learn how to cook," she said. "Your mama's got a fine kitchen. I bet she can cook real good."

I recognized that line of reasoning. "You can try it," I said. "Just tell Mom what you told me."

Stella knocked on the kitchen door and went on in. She didn't reappear, so I guessed Mom was teaching her how to cook.

At three thirty I stuck my head in the kitchen. Stella was chopping apples into tiny pieces while Mom put slices of sweet potatoes into a casserole. Mom looked pleased.

"That's wonderful," she was saying. "I think you have a gift for cooking."

Stella beamed.

"Now we just scatter those over the top," Mom went on, "and slip it into the oven."

I decided I wasn't needed and went into the living room to brood. A couple of minutes later the doorbell rang.

"Are you there, Mary Frances?" Mom yelled.

I acknowledged that I was.

"Would you get the door? My goodness, I'm not even dressed."

I was glad to see somebody needed me for something. I opened the door and got the biggest surprise of the week. There were two people standing on the porch. The one in front was the blond boy I'd seen drinking beer with C.J.

I should have guessed he was Stella's brother. We don't get very many strangers in Monroe. When two show up at once, there's a good chance they're related.

Billy stood back to let his mother enter the house first. I guess she was beautiful. Her hair was bright silver and her eyes were blue, and her eyelashes were about a foot long. She was wearing a black dress and a red belt.

"Hello, honey." She smiled at me. "Your mama home?"

"Yes, ma'am," I said. "You Mrs. Shanks?"

"That I am," she said. "I believe we have been invited to a Thanksgiving do." She stood just inside the door.

"Would you like to come in, please?" I said politely.

"I guess I am in," she said, smiling again.

"Yes," I said, wondering what to say next. I was rescued by my father.

"How do you do," he said, striding up behind me. "I'm Jeffrey Allen. You must be Mrs. Shanks. And this must be Billy."

The men shook hands.

"Please come into the living room," Dad went on. "My wife won't be a minute."

Dad settled Mrs. Shanks into a chair. Billy stood behind her. I fled to the kitchen. There was nobody there but Stella.

"Hey, Stella," I said. "Your folks are here."

"Yeah," Stella said unenthusiastically. "Hey, what am I supposed to do with this can?"

"What is it?"

"Cranberry sauce."

"Open it, I guess," I said facetiously.

"I did," Stella said. "Look at this."

Stella held the can with the open side down. Nothing happened.

I tried it. I even shook it. It was the jelly kind of cranberry sauce and it seemed glued to the can.

We sat down to ponder.

"I think Mom usually opens both ends," I said.

"Why?"

"I don't know," I said, "but it works."

Our can opener is set high on the wall. Stella hooked the can onto it and began to crank. A moment later, the cranberry sauce slid out of the can and smashed onto the floor.

Stella and I looked at it and started to laugh. I grabbed a plate and scooped the solid mass of cranberry sauce onto it.

I was just in time; Mom walked into the kitchen a minute later. "Well, Stella," she said, and then stopped. She looked at the cranberry sauce. "What happened to the cranberry sauce?"

"Nothing," I said quickly. "It just kind of came out of the can like that. Free form."

Mom regarded it for a minute. "I certainly hope you marry a wealthy man," she said. "Stella, your family's here. Would you like to join them?"

"Oh, no, ma'am," Stella said. "Can't I set the table or something?"

"You can both set the table if you'd like," Mom said. "But don't let Mary Frances carry any plates or we'll have to eat off the tablecloth." Mom handed the plates to Stella and the knives and forks to me. "Don't forget the napkins," she said, and left us.

It took us a long time to set the table, because Stella insisted on setting the plates an inch in from the edge of the table, setting the glasses just half an inch past the knives, and twisting the napkins into cones.

"Mama says if a table looks right, don't matter what's on it," Stella explained.

"Well, that table looks right, all right," I assured her.

We took a last look at our festive table and drifted into the living room in time to hear Mrs. Shanks say, ". . . Atlanta."

Mrs. Shanks was leaning back in her chair, a glass of punch in her hand. Billy stood behind the chair. For some odd reason, Pete stood behind Billy.

"What brings you to Monroe?" Dad asked.

"We just liked the sound of it," Mrs. Shanks said and smiled.

"It seems a far way to travel for such a capricious reason," Mom said, doubtfully.

"It might be for some people," Mrs. Shanks said, "but not for the Shankses. Anyway, we were living in Miami at the time."

Mom looked puzzled. "You must have seen a lot of the country."

"That we have. My poor children." She looked up at Billy. "They've never known a real settled home."

"I suppose a settled home life is important," Mom said. "But they say travel broadens the mind. I expect Stella and Billy have learned a lot more than my two. My goodness, we've never been farther afield than Miami."

"I wish I'd never left Atlanta," Mrs. Shanks said with sudden anger. "It wasn't my idea to go flitting around here and there. I'm a simple woman, and I have simple tastes."

Billy put his hand on his mother's shoulder. She continued, but more calmly.

"My husband invented crazy things," she said. "He'd get an idea and drop everything. Spend the food money on outlandish supplies. Trouble was, nobody wanted to buy his inventions."

Billy spoke up. "I don't think anybody's interested in all that, Mama."

"Don't you?" Mrs. Shanks asked, looking up briefly. "I do." She turned back to my parents. "He spent most of his time inventing things, but sooner or later he'd have to go out and get a job. Trouble was, he wasn't good for much, except inventions. The jobs he did—I didn't mind it so much when he sold shoes and magazine subscriptions. But he even worked out in the fields, picking lettuce, just like a nigger. We moved where the work was. The places we lived—all of us living in one room sometimes. The worst was that shack out in the fields." She paused. "He died two years ago. Hit by a truck."

"Oh, dear," Mom said. "It must have been terribly hard to bear."

"That it was. But life must go on," she said brightly. "Billy," she continued, handing him her glass.

Dad rose. "Let me refresh your drink," he said, taking the glass from Billy.

"Somehow we've kept moving," Mrs. Shanks went on, "just like we did when my husband was alive. A woman alone, with children, it's hard to find a place to suit us, you understand."

I could tell Mom didn't understand, but she nodded as if she did.

81

Dad handed Mrs. Shanks a full glass of punch.

"Why, thank you," she said, taking a sip. "Miami suited me. It suited Billy all too well."

I saw Billy stiffen. "I don't think anybody would care about that, Mama," he said. I glanced at Stella. She'd gone as tense as Billy.

"I believe in being honest with people," Mrs. Shanks told Billy. "If you're ashamed of it, you shouldn't have done it." She turned to Mom. "We'd only been there a couple of months when Billy was busted."

There are times when I'm glad Mom has lived a sheltered life. She looked at Billy's arms and legs, trying to see where he'd been busted. Billy was turning red and his fists were clenched.

"He drew a suspended sentence because it was his first offense, far as they knew," Mrs. Shanks went on. "But we thought we'd better leave. Once they've had a boy up before a judge they never leave him alone. Or his family," she added.

There was dead silence. Then Mom spoke. She sounded confused but decidedly sympathetic. "Did they put you in jail, Billy?"

Billy's flush had receded and he'd relaxed a little. "Just until we raised the bail money, ma'am," he said. "I believe I deserved to go to jail. I was breaking the law."

"What exactly was your offense, Billy?" Dad asked.

"I can tell you that," Mrs. Shanks said. "He was smoking that Mexican stuff. What do the kids call it? Grass."

"Grass?" Mom asked, bewildered. "I didn't know anybody smoked grass."

Dad caught on, I was sorry to see. "I hope you've given it up, young man."

"Yes, sir," Billy said. "Anyway, I couldn't smoke it again if I wanted to. There just isn't any grass in Monroe."

"But don't you crave it?" Dad asked.

"No, sir. I just tried it to know what it was like."

I looked at Mom. It was obvious that she still didn't understand why Billy had been busted, but she was convinced he'd been the victim of a grave injustice. "It doesn't seem fair to put a young man in jail," she said finally. "It can ruin his life."

"Lord, it's sure ruined mine," Mrs. Shanks said. "Miami suited me. I don't think Monroe is my kind of place. People don't seem to like a good time here. They're not real friendly, either."

"You'll have to forgive us," Dad said. "This is an ingrown community. We're not used to strangers here, and it takes some time to warm up. I'm sure things will improve as time goes on."

"Oh, yes," Mom chimed in. "Now that we've found you, why, there are a lot of things to do."

Mrs. Shanks looked dubious, so Mom talked harder.

"Now there's the church group and the Junior Chamber of Commerce women's auxiliary, and there's the P.T.A. . . ."

I glanced at Mrs. Shanks. I had the terrible feeling she was going to laugh.

A bell rang in the kitchen. "That's the timer," Mom said apologetically. "I believe dinner is ready."

Dad hadn't even finished carving the turkey when Mrs. Shanks told us that Billy had been busted in Lakeland for stealing a car.

"Whose car was it?" Mom asked.

"My brother's," Mrs. Shanks said. "He was down visiting us from Atlanta. That Billy has no sense."

Mom looked shocked. "Did your brother bring charges?"

"He certainly did," Mrs. Shanks said. "He nearly washed his hands of us."

Mom gazed at Billy, who had gone all red and tense again. "But his own uncle . . ." Mom said.

"Billy," Stella asked suddenly, "why do you have to open both ends of a cranberry-sauce can?"

Billy relaxed. "You tell me."

"I don't know," Stella said. "You open one end and nothing happens. But you punch a hole in the other end and the cranberry sauce just slides right out."

"That's because of air pressure," Billy said.

"Why?"

"Didn't they teach you about vacuums in that fine school of yours?"

"Not yet," Stella said optimistically.

"A vacuum is a complete absence of air," Billy explained. "Nothing moves in a vacuum. It's sealed tight. Now when you open one end of a can of something like cranberry sauce, that sauce is so thick that the air can't get through it to break the vacuum seal. It acts on one surface but not on the other. If you punch a hole in the other end, a bit of air creeps in through the hole. It isn't much, but you know air weighs, oh, point-oh-oh-one-two-nine grams per cubic centimeter. That's enough to break the seal and push the cranberry sauce out."

"Okay," Stella said. "Got it."

"You seem to know a lot about physics," Dad said.

"Not as much as I'd like to know, sir," Billy replied. "Papa taught me a lot."

There are only two things Dad really respects: sound business practices and scientific learning. I suspected Billy's display of scientific learning had won Dad over. I was sure of it a moment later, when Dad offered Billy a drumstick.

Halfway through the meal, Billy turned to Pete, who had managed to seat himself on Billy's right. "How's the team doing?" he asked.

84

Mom, Dad, and I stopped eating. Pete was on a team?

"Getting better," Pete said. "Won by seven points yesterday."

"Did you use that play I gave you?"

"Yeah." Pete grinned. "That was one of the touchdowns. I kicked the extra point."

"No kidding."

"Are you on a football team?" I asked Pete.

Pete ignored me.

"Get your signal system straightened out yet?" Billy asked.

"Nope," Pete said. "Those guys are stupid. You gotta keep hammering away at them."

"Are you on a football team, Pete?" Dad asked.

Pete looked down at his plate. "Yes, sir," he said to his plate.

"What position do you play?" Dad asked.

Pete kept looking at his plate. I could see he was so embarrassed he was speechless. I guess Billy could see it too, because he said, "You don't want to keep a thing that big to yourself, Pete. Can I tell them about it?"

"Okay," Pete told his plate.

"Pete is the captain and quarterback of the First Grade Gators," Billy announced. "I've watched them play. They're good, allowing for their age and inexperience."

"Whom do they play against?" Mom wanted to know.

"They play against the second-grade team, the Tigers." Pete looked up and grinned at Billy. Billy grinned back. "We think that's a stupid name. It's all unofficial, of course. It's not a school activity."

"Well, I never had any idea," Dad said. "All this going on under our noses . . ."

"Pete can run very fast," Billy said hastily. "He can kick a ball a mile. But his passing isn't too great." He looked at Pete. "You know, smart as you are, if you can't throw the ball, you'll never be a quarterback."

"I practice," Pete said.

"I know you do," Billy said. "But while the season's on, you don't have much time. Maybe after Christmas we can get in a few afternoons a week."

"Have you been coaching the team?" Dad asked, ready to believe anything.

"Just Pete, sir," Billy said. "Well, now and again I give the team a few pointers. A few plays."

"But when do you have the time?" Mom asked.

"Time's something I've got plenty of, ma'am," Billy said. "I've got all my afternoons free."

"Billy works mornings," Pete said suddenly.

"That's right," Billy confirmed.

"Where did you play football, Billy?" Dad asked.

"I've played it on and off just about all over the state, sir," Billy said. "I played in Lakeland when we lived there, and Plant City one season, and a few places you've probably never heard of."

"What position did you play?"

"Safety, sir."

"We thought they'd offer Billy a scholarship to the University of Florida, he was that good," Mrs. Shanks said suddenly. "Two years ago he made the Florida state all-scholastic team. But that stupid thing he did in Lakeland kept following him. They never let a boy forget."

Nobody could think of an answer to that, so we finally gave up trying. "Ah," Mom said. "Have some more sweet potato, Billy, Mrs. Shanks. Stella made it."

"No," exclaimed Mrs. Shanks. "When did that child learn to cook?"

"About an hour ago," Stella said.

"You've been holding out on us, Stella," Billy said, grinning at her.

"She seems to have a gift for cooking," Mom said.

Stella beamed.

All this sweetness and light was getting to me. "May I be excused to feed the dogs?" I asked Dad. "This is their dinner hour."

"I think they can wait half an hour," Dad said.

"I don't know," I said. "They might break the gate down."

"I'll tell you what we'll do," Dad said. "You wait until we've finished dinner and we'll all feed the dogs together."

I know when I'm beaten. "Yes, sir," I said, and gritted my teeth through the next half hour.

Finally we were all assembled in the backyard, surrounded by a restless horde of hungry dogs. Mrs. Shanks looked aghast at the scene before her.

"Nine dogs," she said. "Lord. They must be a lot of trouble."

"Not really," Mom said. "Except for Scrappy, they tend to look after one another."

I had emptied a sack of dry feed into the old plastic dishpan that served as a common feeding bowl. After adding water from the hose, I set the bowl down and the dogs crowded around. Scrappy tried to make his way through but the other dogs wouldn't let him. Finally he stood on the outskirts of the group, growling.

I grabbed Scrappy by the collar. "Come on," I said, dragging him into the kitchen. Stella and Billy followed. I reached Scrappy's bowl off the drainboard. "Here you go," I said, putting it down.

Stella had seen this performance before, but Billy hadn't. He stood transfixed as Scrappy looked around, growling to left and right, and suddenly rushed the bowl and ate the dog food, growling all the time.

"That's a most unpleasant dog," Mrs. Shanks remarked, coming into the kitchen.

"It's not his fault," I said.

"You ever see anything like that, Billy?" Stella asked.

Billy admitted he hadn't. "Poor little guy," he said. "I think he needs a place of his own."

"What's that?" I asked.

"Some dogs can live in groups," Billy said, "and some dogs can't. They need their own territory."

"I believe you're right," Mom said. She'd brought the empty dishpan back. "Dogs gone wild seem to form packs. But now and again you see a lone dog living out in the country, perfectly happy catching rabbits on his own." She turned to Mrs. Shanks. "I've tried to find a home for him," she said, "but nobody seems to want him. I don't suppose you'd like to take him in?"

"Lord, no," Mrs. Shanks said. "I've got my hands full looking after these two." She smiled at Stella and Billy.

The Shanks family left soon afterward.

"What a nice boy," Mom said.

"A fine youngster," Dad agreed.

"Poor child," Mom said. "His uncle sounds like a thoroughly detestable man. I suppose stealing his car was Billy's way of getting back at him."

"Anybody can make a mistake," Dad agreed.

I listened in amazement. Billy was a convicted dope fiend and car thief and maybe an alcoholic as well. Normally, I would have pointed this out. But I discovered that I preferred leaving my parents in their tolerant state. Whatever his faults, Billy knew a lot about football and dogs, and that, I realized, made up for almost anything.

8

The Monroe School Varsity's annual Thanksgiving Classic exhibition was scheduled for Saturday afternoon. I hadn't planned to attend. But at the last minute, I decided it might be interesting to watch Ronnie and George in action, keeping the football team up to scratch.

As I hiked past Second Street on the way to the practice field, it occurred to me that Stella might want to come along.

She did. We hurried back down the street.

"It probably won't be very exciting," I said. "They just show off their new plays. Hey, what's the matter?"

Stella had stopped by the gas pump outside C.J.'s. "There's something funny," she said.

"I don't notice anything."

"C.J. He's not on his bench."

That's when we noticed that the door was closed as well. We went up and banged on it and the sound echoed in the hot, heavy air.

"Guess nobody's there," Stella said.

"That store's been open six days a week since I can remember," I pointed out.

"Maybe we ought to go on out to the house and see what's the matter."

"I don't think that's a very good idea."

"Why not?"

"It's pretty far out, for one thing," I said. "It's practically in North Monroe."

"You don't sound real enthusiastic," Stella said.

"Well, if I go over there, Dad will say I'm being nosy," I explained.

"Nothing nosy about it," Stella objected. "It's neighborly, is all."

"Anyway, C.J. will think we're crazy," I said. "You can go if you want to. I'm going to watch the football exhibition."

Stella stood still a moment. "I guess you're right," she said finally. "Come on, we better get moving."

On Monday afternoon, Stella accepted my invitation for milk and Oreos. The store was still closed when we walked past it.

"I just know something's wrong," Stella said. "Something real serious."

"You sound as if you know something."

"I don't," Stella assured me. "I just have a feeling."

Mom wandered into the kitchen a few minutes after we arrived. This was most unusual. Mom turns the kitchen over to the younger generation every afternoon and only comes in when she hears something crash.

She looked dazed. "I suppose you girls have heard the news."

"War?"

Mom shot me a severe look. "Your levity is unwarranted."

When Mom begins to talk like Dad, it's a good sign she's upset. She sat at the table and I poured her a glass of milk.

"Callie Caldwell had a heart attack Saturday morning," Mom said finally. "She's dead."

"Mrs. C.J.?" I cried, startled.

Mom nodded. She told us that Emily hadn't been in class that morning. The principal had called her teachers together and explained the reason for Emily's absence. Half an hour later, during the class break, the high school had been buzzing with the news.

News usually travels through Monroe at roughly the speed of sound. Yet nobody had known anything about Mrs. C.J.'s death until Monday morning, two days later.

"I suppose we didn't hear about it because the Caldwells live so far out of the way," Mom said, "and Callie was taken ill at home. At least she didn't die in the store, standing on her feet, waiting on that drunken husband of hers. I suppose one can take comfort from that."

Everybody was acting odd that day. Most afternoons, Pete's sorties into the kitchen would do credit to a herd of rampaging elephants. Today he came in so quietly that nobody noticed him. I believe he must have come in just about the time Stella was saying, "She had dizzy spells."

"That's right, Stella," Mom said. "C.J. can't say he didn't know his wife was ill." She paused and took a sip of milk. "He killed her, you know. That sorry man worked her to death."

Pete dropped his football suddenly and the three of us looked up, startled. We stared at Pete, and he stared at us, and then he grabbed his football and ran out of the kitchen.

"That child ought to make more noise," Mom said irritably. "I wonder how much he heard."

I assured Mom that he'd just come in, but I was pretty sure he'd heard more than enough.

The store remained shut until after the funeral the next day. Dad closed his shop and went along to represent the family.

"There must have been a hundred people there," he reported at dinner.

"Poor Callie," Mom said.

"Do you remember old Joe Becker? And the Richardsons? Even the Harringtons came down from Jacksonville. And I suppose a fair number of your pupils stayed home today."

"About fifty," Mom said. "Emily's very popular."

"So was Callie at that age," Dad remarked.

"Did you used to know Mrs. C.J.?" I asked.

"Well, you know, she was a local girl," Mom said. "Monroe was smaller in those days. Everyone knew everyone else. Callie was so pretty," she added, smiling.

"Callie was also rather scatterbrained," Dad said dryly, "if I may be forgiven for seeming to speak ill of the dead."

"I suppose you could put it that way," Mom said, "but she was pretty and pleasant enough. Everyone liked her. And then one day . . ." Mom's voice trailed off.

"And then one day what?" I prompted.

"One day," Mom said, "C.J. came roaring into town on the back of a big red Harley-Davidson. No one ever found out where he came from."

"You can believe that the good ladies of Monroe put their hearts and souls into the investigation," Dad commented.

Mom continued, "We knew nothing about his family. But it was as plain as day that he had no education. He was a thoroughly graceless individual. It seemed to me that he took delight in shocking people."

"How?"

"There were little things," Mom said. "Do you remember?" She turned to Dad. "C.J. went to church just once, and he belched—excuse me—throughout the entire sermon. I admit that sounds funny, but it wasn't. He used to drink heavily, even then, and he would walk through the streets of Monroe in the middle of the night singing the most outrageous songs. And then," she added, "he used to pick fights. He picked a fight one day with my cousin Wellington. Wellington gave up almost at once. He was no fool. But C.J. professed not to hear him. He continued fighting until he'd broken Wellington's arm. I heard it crack. I think C.J. enjoyed hurting people.

"Callie adored him," Mom continued, "and one day they eloped to Georgia. She was only sixteen. C.J. must have been at least thirty." She paused. "It broke her father's heart."

"Now, Margaret," Dad said.

"Oh, I know, Callie would never have amounted to much," Mom admitted. "But C.J. made her life so hard. Oh, dear," she said, as a tear splashed into her soup. "Excuse me." And she hurried into the kitchen.

Stella and I went to C.J.'s store on Wednesday afternoon to pay Emily our respects. We'd intended to pay C.J. our respects, too, but he was nowhere in sight.

We found Emily in her mother's place behind the counter.

"Good afternoon," Emily said. "Orange sodas?"

"Oh, no," I said hastily. "We just came by to tell you how sorry we are about your mother."

"She was a real kind lady," Stella said. "I'm sure going to miss her."

"She was," Emily said, and she tried to smile. It didn't work. "Here," she said, "let me offer you something." She walked slowly to the cold case, pulled out an orange soda and opened it. "You two can share that. On the house," she added, handing the soda to Stella.

"Thank you," I said.

"Mama really liked you girls," Emily said. "I don't mind you much myself," she added, and then she managed to smile.

"Where's your papa?" Stella asked.

"I don't know," Emily said. "I think he must be home getting drunk."

without meaning to. We tend to be respectful in

Monroe, and Emily's lived here all her life. About the time we learn about "sir" and "ma'am," we learn the Fifth Commandment.

"I find it difficult to honor my father," Emily said, reading my thoughts. "Monroe really prepares us for life. We've got guidelines for every situation. Work hard and ye shall be rewarded. Go to church and ye shall be saved. Don't smoke grass or steal cars and people will respect you. Honor thy father and the world will call you blessed." She stopped. "I can't honor a man I don't respect, even if he is my father. Could you?"

"I don't know," I said.

Stella handed the soda bottle over to me. "I guess I'd try to stay out of his way."

Emily sat down. "That won't work anymore," she said. "Papa's taken me out of school."

I banged the soda bottle down on the counter. "What?"

"Six months before graduation," Emily said. "He wants me to run the store. Leaves him free to drink beer and whiskey all day."

"He does that anyway," Stella said.

"He doesn't want me to graduate," Emily said. "He's acting like a madman. I guess he didn't expect Mama to die." She stopped for a moment and then went on. "He seems to hate everybody, especially me. I suppose I ought to try to understand him, but I can't. He wants to ruin my life. He can do it, too. Billy . . ." Then she stopped.

"What about Billy?" Stella prompted.

"Don't tell Billy," Emily said. "I don't know what he'll do."

"I won't tell him," Stella promised. "I guess he'll find out soon enough, though. The minute . . ."

Somebody bumped hard into the side of the doorway. We looked up. C.J. was staring at the doorjamb as if he were seeing it for the first time.

Suddenly he whipped around. "What you kids doing here?" he growled.

"The store's open, Papa," Emily said. "Go on home."

"I got a right to be here," C.J. said, in a funny, whining voice. "I got a right to be here!" he yelled at us. "Go on, git!"

Stella and I just stood there. C.J. was blocking the door.

"I told y'all to git!" he yelled, raising his hand.

I was getting nervous, and I guess I reacted like a little girl. "We can't, sir," I said. "You're blocking the door."

I don't think anybody had bothered to call C.J. "sir" in years. He smiled. "You're a good girl," he said. "Ain't grown much lately. Now git!" he yelled, moving out of the way.

Stella flashed Emily a smile and ran out. I waved to Emily and followed.

We stopped by the gas pump.

"Billy?" I said to Stella.

"Listen, don't say anything," Stella said. "Billy doesn't like people poking around his life. Let's go on to my house." She headed down Second Street without waiting for an answer. I followed.

"I won't say anything," I said as we walked along. "I don't even know anything."

"I guess you noticed Billy hanging around C.J. all the time, drinking beer and all," Stella said.

"Well, I guess I have."

"You never said anything," Stella said. "I thought that was real nice of you."

"I didn't want to embarrass you," I said, growing embarrassed. "Anyway, Dad's always talking about how the ladies in Monroe would put the CIA to shame, the way they find things out, and I guess I try to mind my own business. Sometimes," I added.

"Well, you know how C.J. doesn't let Emily go out on dates with anybody."

"I didn't know that."

"Well, he doesn't. So Emily has been going out with Billy secretly. The way it works, you know, C.J. goes home from the store early sometimes. Well, he doesn't exactly go home. I think he goes to a poker game. Anyway, that's what Mrs. C.J. said." We'd reached Stella's house and we sat on the steps.

"Where did they go?"

"Nowhere," Stella said. "Emily was afraid her papa would see them. So what they did, soon as C.J. went off to his poker game, Emily would slip out and come over here. She and Billy, they'd just sit in his room and talk. Sometimes I gave them peanut-butter sandwiches. Then when Mrs. C.J. was ready to close up the store, why, she'd come to fetch Emily."

I was speechless. I had the feeling I'd been living in a private backwater of my own. "So Mrs. C.J. knew about it too," I finally managed to say.

"Yeah," Stella said. "Everybody knew but C.J. Now Billy doesn't mind sneaking around. In fact, he used to like it. But he says it's different this time. He really likes Emily. I think he wants to marry her. That's why he's always hanging around C.J. He had the idea maybe he could win C.J.'s affection and respect, and C.J. would give them his blessing, and then Billy and Emily, they could see each other out in the open."

"What's C.J. got against Billy?"

"I'll get us something to eat," Stella said. She disappeared inside the house, leaving me to figure it out myself.

I had it worked out by the time she reappeared.

"It isn't just Billy," I said. "C.J. doesn't want Emily to marry anybody. He just wants her to run the store."

"Right," Stella said. "Even if Billy had a lot of money, C.J. wouldn't want Emily to marry him. And Billy hasn't got a dime. You know where he works? He's a bag boy mornings at the supermarket. He works for tips. He's got to feed him and me both out of that. Mama keeps her own money.

"But that's not all," Stella went on. "Billy knows how much Emily wants to be a nurse. He told me he'd wait for her till she finished nursing school, if that's what she wants. Man," she said. "I don't know what Billy's going to do when he finds out C.J.'s taken Emily out of school."

On Thursday night, Mom reported that the high school was in an uproar. C.J. had sent a letter to the principal announcing that Emily wouldn't be coming back.

The principal told Mom he'd be calling on C.J.

"He thinks he can talk some sense into him," Mom said sadly at dinner. "Nobody's ever been able to talk sense into that man."

"He'll probably be drunk," I said.

"You mind your manners," Dad said.

"He was sure drunk yesterday," I added. "He threw Stella and me out of the store."

"I don't blame him," Dad said. "You ought to show a little respect for your elders."

"Some elders you just can't respect," I pointed out.

"You might try harder," Dad said.

"Can I try with Miss Holloway?" I asked. "C.J.'s just a little too much to ask."

"Don't be smart," Dad said. "There are certain rules that make it possible for men to live together in some degree of harmony. We all live by rules worked out over the centuries and found to make life a finer thing. Good manners make life just that much more pleasant."

"We've got guidelines for every situation in Monroe," I said glumly.

"I suppose we do," Dad agreed. "Don't laugh at those guidelines, Mary Frances. If the idea of respecting your elders is a good one, then it should be applied right down the line. You'll start out sneering at C.J., and you'll end up sneering at your mother. That's what guidelines are for."

"That doesn't leave much room for originality,"I objected.

"I expect you'll find some," Mom said. "Now then, why don't you think of an original way to get these dirty dishes into the kitchen."

"Pete could carry them," I suggested.

Pete glowered at me.

"This family is beyond originality," I said, getting up to clear the table.

Mr. Perkins, the principal, came by the store the next afternoon. Stella and I were standing silently at the counter drinking orange sodas when Ronnie sped through the door.

"Mr. Perkins is on the way," he said. "Mind if I have a Nehi, Emily? Don't get up—I'll get it."

A few moments later, we heard the slow, heavy tread of Mr. Perkins, who joined C.J. on his bench. C.J. called to Emily for beers. Mr. Perkins declined. Emily remained at her counter.

"I was very surprised to read your letter, Mr. Caldwell," Mr. Perkins started.

"I expanded my business," C.J. answered. "Got to put all my resources into it."

"I don't quite see what that has to do with Emily's education," Mr. Perkins said.

"Emily now, she's one of my resources," C.J. said. His voice took on the strange, whining quality I'd heard on Wednesday. "I can't help it," he said. "I got this franchise from the gas company. I got more work than I can handle on my own. I got to mind the gas pump. I got to see the store's run proper. I can't be in two places at once."

"Surely you can hire a boy to run the store?" the principal suggested.

"Don't have to," C.J. said triumphantly. "I got my little girl here to help her papa out."

"Do you think that's fair, Mr. Caldwell?" Mr. Perkins asked. "She's one of the best students we've ever had. She'll graduate in another six months, and with her grades any nursing school in the country would be proud to accept her."

C.J. didn't answer for a minute or two. When he began to speak, I glanced at Emily. She looked terrified.

"That little girl," C.J. crooned, "for seventeen years I been feeding her, I been clothing her, I been giving her a roof over her head. Her mama wanted her to get a fine education. Look at me," he said, his voice rising. "I never had no fine education. I ain't doing so bad. But it was the law. The law says you got to keep your child in school until she's sixteen." He paused. Then he said slowly, "She's seventeen now, Mr. Perkins, and she's had all the fine education she's gonna get. It's time she started to help her papa out. I need her in the store. You take care of your long-hair hippie students," he said. "I'll take care of my family. She ain't going back to school, and there ain't nothing you can do about it."

"We'll see about that," Mr. Perkins said.

"Just you do," C.J. said. "And don't come around here no more or I'll set the police on you."

We heard Mr. Perkins leaving, then C.J. calling Emily.

Emily walked to the cold case, took out a beer, opened it, and took it outside to C.J. We three looked at each other.

"Clearly," Ronnie said, "something must be done."

"Do you have a plan?" I asked hopefully.

"Not at the moment," Ronnie said. "I'll try to think of something." He looked straight at Stella. "And you're not going to talk me out of it this time."

"I won't," Stella said. "Come on."

Stella marched out of the store and darted across the street. We followed her through the vacant lot. She stopped at the first clearing, looked around, and sat on the root of a tree. We followed suit.

"I wanted to make sure nobody could hear us," Stella explained. "Look, I was going to do this by myself but it's not good enough. I guess I can trust y'all."

"Stella," Ronnie said, "you can trust me to the ends of the earth. I would gladly lay down my life for you."

"You would?" I said.

"Why not?" Ronnie answered. "I believe I've done it before. A mere three months ago . . ."

"You don't have to do much," Stella interrupted. "Not risk your life or anything. Billy knows about a hiding place in that store with a lot of money in it. He doesn't know how much. He thinks it's C.J.'s poker winnings. You know, C.J.'s like that. He'd want to have ready cash at hand all the time, in case he wanted to play poker or buy whiskey, and he'd want it secret so Mrs. C.J. couldn't ask him about it."

"Would you like us to steal it?" Ronnie asked in an offhand fashion.

"No. Billy's going to do that. He figures he can use the money," Stella explained, "to elope to Georgia with Emily, where nobody cares how old they are, and then Emily can finish school and go on to nurses' school."

"I suppose Emily doesn't know anything about this?" I said.

"Billy would die if she knew," Stella said simply. "She'd never speak to him."

"I don't know," I said. "She seems pretty bitter lately."

"Basically," Ronnie said, "Emily is a very moral person. I don't believe she'd countenance stealing."

100

"Okay," I said, convinced. "I hope Billy makes it. I mean, I don't approve of stealing either, but stealing from C.J. . . ." I didn't finish the sentence because I couldn't. I had the feeling I would have a hard time explaining my reasoning to my father, but fortunately he wasn't around at the moment.

"He wants me to help him," Stella said. "He wants me to be the lookout. Now C.J.'s is next to that lot and there's that big tree, and it's got two entrances, and I don't think I can watch everywhere all at once. Can you help me? I wouldn't ask," she said apologetically, "but it's for Billy."

"Of course we'll help," Ronnie said. "What about it, Mary Frances?"

Wishing Billy luck was one thing. Helping him steal was another. I hesitated.

"That's okay," Stella said, when I didn't answer right away. "Ronnie and I can do it."

"You and Ronnie can't do a thing alone," I said angrily. "You need me. You need at least four more people. Think about it."

They thought about it. Then Ronnie said, "I think we can do it with five people. We don't really need six. I'll get George."

"Why should George help?" Stella objected. "It's not fair."

"George is okay," Ronnie said. "He'll help. How about Alison?"

"I don't know," I said. "She's pretty straight."

"So are you," Ronnie said. "So's Stella. We can't let C.J. ruin Emily's life."

"You're right," I said. "I'll ask her. She'll probably say no."

But she didn't when I told her about the plan an hour later. In fact, she laughed.

"Alison!" I said, shocked. "It's a sin to steal."

"It certainly is," Alison agreed. "There are times you must

101

fight fire with fire. I've been waiting for years to get back at C.J."

"I guess you have," I said. "But somehow I didn't think you'd want to do this."

"I don't think I could actually steal," Alison said thoughtfully, "even from C.J. But I could be a lookout. That's all right."

"I just don't understand your attitude," I said, completely puzzled.

"Look, Mary Frances," Alison said. "We've known each other all our lives. Since we were tiny children I've been a paragon of virtues. Isn't that true? I play in the school band. I don't waste my time hanging around drinking orange sodas. I'm a perfect little lady. And I'm smart, too. Every year, either I'm at the top of the class or Ronnie is. We seem to take turns."

"That's true," I agreed. "And I know how much you hate it. Remember the time you put on my old torn dungarees and we went up to North Monroe and stood around a soda shop, just so you could get the feel of it?"

"Now, I don't think I'd like to do that all the time," Alison said. "But it would be nice sometimes. And you know I can't. Because of C.J."

That took me by surprise. "C.J.?"

"C.J.," Alison repeated. "You know how my mother's always going on about setting an example. I have to represent all black people everywhere. Otherwise people will be prejudiced and look down on us, and we'll have to step into the gutter when white folks walk by, smile all the time, and eat chicken necks. Now I have only encountered one case of prejudice in all of Monroe, and that's C.J., and I've never been anywhere else. When is Billy robbing the store?"

"Eleven o'clock tonight," I told her.

"Eleven!" Alison exclaimed. "How does he expect me to get out of the house at eleven o'clock at night?"

"He doesn't expect anything like that," I reminded her. "He thinks Stella's his only lookout. He doesn't know about the rest of us."

"Don't worry," Alison said. "I'll be there, if I have to climb out of my bedroom window."

9

Much later, when it was all over, we compared notes. Alison, George, and I climbed out of our bedroom windows. In George's case, that was pretty impressive. His bedroom is on the second floor. I still don't know how he did it. Maybe he slid down one of those marble pillars.

Ronnie sneaked out the back door of his house. And Stella just strolled out of her front door in time to meet all of us in the first clearing at ten to eleven.

Ronnie assumed charge of the operation, assigning a post to each lookout. Stella was stationed across from the front door of the store, while I was put slightly into the vacant lot, across from the back door. George was told to melt into the shadows under the tree. Alison was positioned looking south along the road, at the edge of the lot. Ronnie would look up Second Street.

"Wait a minute," Alison said. "That's silly. I can melt into a shadow without even trying. Besides, George can sprint down the road faster than I can if he sees somebody coming."

George liked that. "Okay," he said. "We'll swap posts."

Ronnie was annoyed. "I've worked this plan out very carefully."

"Not carefully enough," Alison snapped back. "What's the signal if we see somebody coming?"

"Billy told me to whistle twice, real sharp, like this," Stella said, and she demonstrated.

I got a cold feeling in the small of my back. I can't whistle. I'd never had any call to whistle in public; that's one social grace girls in Monroe are expected to forgo. Nobody knew I couldn't whistle. But I knew. I'd tried it many times over the years, in the privacy of my room.

I hoped fervently that I wouldn't see anybody.

"Okay," Ronnie said. "Every man to his post."

We scattered.

People think of funny things while sitting at the edge of a vacant lot at night staring at a dark store. The stars were out and the air was warm and heavy. There wasn't any breeze at all, and I thought about how glad I was mosquitoes stayed out of Monroe in the wintertime. Something bit me on the leg just the same, and I thought about what it could be while I scratched the bite. It wasn't a green snake, because they don't bite. It wasn't a spider, either, for the same reason. Maybe it was a scorpion. I tried to remember whether a scorpion sting was always fatal, and I noticed somebody sneaking up to C.J.'s back door. My hand stopped in midscratch and then I tried to whistle.

I failed lamentably. An instant later, I recognized Billy.

I felt like a fool. Lucky for all of us I couldn't whistle. And then I thought, Wouldn't it be funny if nobody else can whistle either. I tried to remember whether I'd ever heard any of the others whistling. Stella, well, yes, she'd whistled tonight. Ronnie, now, did he ever whistle? At the dogs, maybe? Last summer, when he was working out new signals for the team, what was that he'd said? Something about two sets of numbers and a whistle, and then . . .

And then suddenly I heard a crash and a yell and the lights went on in the store. I heard somebody hollering. I started to run toward the store. I'd reached the gas pump when I recognized the voice. It was C.J.

"Going after my cache, were you, boy?" C.J. yelled. "I'll fix you good. You ain't going to have no arm left, boy. C.J. looks after his own."

Stella sped past me and hammered on the front door.

"Feel that, boy?" I heard C.J. snarl. "I'm an old man, but I got forty-fifty pounds on you."

Stella was frantic. She raced around the side of the store and darted into the back door.

"Stop it! Stop it!" we heard her scream. And then suddenly we were all there, huddled around the gas pump.

"Stay here," Ronnie said, and ran through the back door. George followed.

Alison and I looked at each other.

"In for a penny, in for a pound," Alison said.

"What?" I asked, but she flashed me a reckless kind of smile and sped off after the boys without answering.

I followed.

C.J. had Billy's arm twisted behind him; he was holding him by the jackknifed arm like a shield. In his free hand C.J. held an old shotgun, its barrel resting in his armpit.

Now it's one thing to see guns on television and in the movies, and another thing to come face to face with them. We'd all seen what a shotgun could do out in the swamps where C.J. and his friends hunted rabbits, and the sight of the gun kept us all a few feet away.

George had spread his arms in front of him, his big hands hanging useless. Stella was screaming. Ronnie was trying to reason.

"You can't go around attacking people, C.J.," he said. "We were just passing by and we heard the noise."

"Just passing my foot!" C.J. said. "Y'all look to me like a gang of hippie thieves and I got your leader." He smiled. "Got me a little surprise for Emily." He flung Billy at us.

"Ain't gonna shoot nobody," he said. "Just gonna call the police chief."

He pulled the shotgun up level so it was pointed at us, and then he lifted the phone off the hook. He dialed with his free hand and put the phone to his ear. "That you, John?" he said, and paused. "Well, fetch him for me."

"What's going on?" Billy whispered to Stella.

"There were too many directions to watch," Stella said.

"No, sir, I want the chief," C.J. said into the phone.

"We wanted to help," I offered. "We all hate C.J."

Billy swung around and looked at me grimly.

"That's no reason to rob a man," he said.

"Billy, you feeling all right?" Stella asked.

"I've got a feeling I'm not getting off with probation this time," he said.

"We could all rush him," Stella said. "There's five of us. Six. To one of him."

"Violence isn't going to get us anywhere," Billy said.

"It could get us out of here," Ronnie pointed out.

Billy didn't seem to hear him. "I didn't figure on involving a bunch of kids," he said. "It's okay for me. Everybody thinks I'm a criminal anyway."

Stella froze at the sound of the word. "They're gonna put you in jail, Billy," she whispered.

"I guess so," Billy said. He stood thinking a minute.

C.J. raised his voice. "That's right, John. Caught a hippie trying to rob my store."

"You kids have got to stay out of it," Billy said. "That's a good story you told, Ronnie. You stick to it. You hear?" and he stared at each of us. "Just passing by."

"At eleven at night?" Alison said.

C.J. raised his voice. "Got a whole pack of kids here, John. Guess they're in on it." Then he called out our names, one by one. "That's right, John. Better hurry out here." And he hung up the phone.

"Just take a seat," he said, "and don't think the chief's going to believe that 'just passing by' tale of yours. If nothing else, I'll get the pack of you for trespassing. Don't think I need this anymore," he said, and put the shotgun under the counter. "Chief knows you're here. You really done it this time."

We really had done it this time. Chief of Police Patterson was accompanied by a patrol car full of policemen, and they all crowded into the store to hear C.J. tell his story.

"I was sleeping in the back room," C.J. said, "just sleeping light. My little girl, Miss High and Mighty Emily, she locked me out of the house. Said I was drunk. You ever see me drunk, John?" he asked the police chief.

Chief Patterson didn't answer.

C.J. continued: "I'm sleeping in the back room when I see the thief creep past me. He goes on into the store. I grab my gun here and I wait, and then very carefully I look through the door. This boy here, he's worked his way back of the cold case. Got his hand right on this brick here when I hit him good."

"What's behind the brick, C.J.?" Chief Patterson wanted to know.

"Got a little cache there, John," C.J. said. "You know how it is. Callie and my little girl, they don't like a man to have a little fun. Count every penny. A man needs some money his womenfolk don't know about."

"Good place to put a cache," the chief noted. "How'd you know about it, boy?"

"I just guessed, sir," Billy said, and shut his mouth tight.

Chief Patterson looked at Billy with a quizzical sort of expression. "I doubt that, boy. Did Emily tell you?"

"No sir," Billy said. "Emily knows nothing about this. She'd never countenance it."

Then I got that funny chill in the small of my back again. I could think of a six-year-old boy who might very well countenance robbery. On and off, every day for weeks, Pete had been sitting behind the cold case, waiting for the mouse. Of course he'd fiddled around a bit with this and that. And one day he'd pulled at a brick and it had come loose. . . .

I tried not to think about it.

"I don't care where he found out about my cache," C.J. went on peevishly. "I want to charge this boy with breaking and entering and robbing my store. Trying to rob my store," he corrected himself. "And conspiracy, I reckon. The kids were lookouts."

"How'd you get in, boy?" the chief asked Billy.

"The back door was unlocked," Billy said.

"That true, C.J.?"

C.J. got a crafty look in his eyes. "Couldn't be," he said. "I locked it. The boy musta picked the lock."

"Go see about that, Jimmy," Chief Patterson told one of his men, who went into the back room. We waited uncomfortably for him to return.

"No signs of a forced entry, sir," Officer Jimmy reported, coming back. "No scratches around the lock."

"Picked the lock," C.J. insisted. "Think I'm fool enough to leave my store open in the middle of the night?"

"We'll have to call it trespassing, C.J.," the chief said.

"I want to charge this boy with breaking and entering," C.J. said stubbornly.

"Listen here, C.J." the chief said. "You want this boy punished?"

"This boy," C.J. said, "he's been hanging around, playing up to me, and all the time he's after my little girl. Think I don't know that, Billy? You lost her now, boy. She ain't gonna waste her time with no convict."

"Trespassing and attempted larceny," the chief said patiently. "We'll have to take you in and book you, boy."

Stella set up a wail. Billy turned to glare at her; she caught his look and her sobs died down into sniffles.

"Now about these kids," Chief Patterson said. "You kids really lookouts?"

Ronnie explained that we'd been just passing by. We confirmed his story.

"I doubt that," the chief said. "What about it, boy?" he asked Billy.

"They had nothing to do with it, sir," Billy said. "Why, aside from my sister and one or two others, I don't even know these kids. Never saw them before."

Chief Patterson considered for a moment. "Guess we'd have trouble proving conspiracy, C.J., if they stick to their story," he said.

C.J. went wild. "Trespassing," he yelled. "They're trespassing on my premises."

"Well, now, C.J.," the chief said, "we'd have a hard time proving they didn't hear all the noise and run in to help."

I was beginning to relax when Chief Patterson's next words hit me in the stomach.

"Do your parents know you make a habit of wandering the streets in the middle of the night?" he asked kindly.

"I believe they do," Ronnie said.

"We'll see about that," the chief said. "Now I think maybe it's not a good idea to let you kids wander on home by yourselves. It's pretty late for youngsters. My men will see you get delivered safely to your parents' waiting arms. You'd better come along with me, boy," he said to Billy. "We'll just drive on down to the station house. Good thing you called, C.J.

You can come along tomorrow and sign the complaint when we get the charges sorted out."

Billy and Chief Patterson strolled out to the patrol car while C.J. watched them, glowering, from the doorway.

The policeman called Jimmy grabbed me by the elbow.

"You don't have to go to all that trouble," I said. "I only live a couple of blocks away. I'll get home all right."

"Let's just see you do," Officer Jimmy said. And with his hand firmly on my elbow we walked the two blocks to Poinsettia.

The dogs began to bark the instant Officer Jimmy rang the doorbell. It took Dad a full four minutes to get to the door, and by that time lights were going on in half the houses on the block. Officer Jimmy hustled me quickly inside.

"Mr. Allen," he said to Dad. "Sorry to disturb you so late, sir. Is this your daughter?"

"It appears to be," Dad said. "It's kind of you to bring her home. May I ask where you found her?"

"I'll tell you all about it, Dad," I broke in hastily. "I'm sure Officer Jimmy's in a hurry."

Officer Jimmy looked at me a little sadly. "I'm sorry, Mary Frances, chief's instructions," he said. He turned back to Dad. "We found your daughter in C. J. Caldwell's store. Seems there was a robbery. A youngster named Billy Shanks tried to rob the store."

"Oh, dear," we heard from the dining-room doorway. Mom was standing there, looking as if she'd been hit. "Poor Billy."

"Evening, ma'am," Officer Jimmy said. "I'm real sorry about all this. Your daughter and a bunch of kids were there when we arrived. There is no evidence we can see that the kids were in on it." He stressed the word "evidence."

"Were you involved in this affair, Mary Frances?" Dad asked, fixing me with a nasty look.

112

"If you'll excuse me, sir," Officer Jimmy said, "I'd better be getting along to the station house. Good night, ma'am."

Mom showed Officer Jimmy to the door while Dad and I stood motionless, glaring at each other like a couple of hawks. When the door closed, Dad looked up at Mom.

"That's curious," he said.

"Yes, it is," Mom agreed. "He gave the impression that he didn't want to know whether Mary Frances was involved or not."

"Excuse me, sir," I said. "I think maybe he thought I'd lie anyway."

Dad turned back to glare at me. "And are you intending to lie?"

"No, sir," I said. "I know when I've been caught. I knew about the robbery this afternoon. I think I'm an accessory." And I told them about it.

Mom's interest kept straying to Billy. "How shocked he must have been when you all piled into the store," she said once. And "I wonder how he would have explained the money to Emily." And, finally, "But how do you suppose he knew about the cache?"

"I told him," said a tough little voice from the dining-room doorway. The three of us swiveled around and stared at Pete, standing straight and proud.

Dad was the first to recover.

"I don't like to doubt your word, son," he said, "but I can't see how you'd know any more than Billy would."

"I knew," Pete insisted. "I knew a long time. I told Billy a long time ago. When C.J. killed Mrs. C.J."

"Now nobody's killed Mrs. C.J.," Dad said sternly. "She died and went to heaven in the natural course of events, the way all of us will someday."

"Killed her," Pete said.

"It was a manner of speaking," Mom told Pete gently.

"What's going on here?" Dad asked.

Mom recounted our conversation about Mrs. C.J. that Pete had overheard on Monday. "You see how quiet he can be," she ended. "No way to tell how long he's been standing here tonight."

"A fine state of affairs," Dad growled. "My children are criminals and my wife's taken up membership in the Monroe ladies' broadcasting association."

"Yes," Mom admitted. "It was foolish. But that hardly solves our problem. I suppose we ought to have a talk with Dave."

I had the feeling I'd just been hit in the stomach again. Dave is my Uncle Dave, the county prosecutor, and he has a highly developed sense of sin. He thinks people ought to be put in jail for talking back to their parents. We'd never get out of it.

"Wait a minute," I said. "He'll put Pete in jail as an accessory before the fact."

"I don't think he'll go that far," Mom said.

"I don't care," Pete said. "Serves him right."

"I daresay it did," Mom agreed, understanding immediately. "C.J.'s a thoroughly dishonest and despicable person. But two wrongs don't make a right."

I'd been hoping Mom wouldn't say that. "What about the others?" I said. "This will ruin Alison."

That brought Mom up short. She turned to Dad. "What do you think?"

"I think that this is a moral issue I'm not prepared to solve at one in the morning," Dad said. "I suggest we sleep on it."

We slept on it.

Just before I drifted off, I tried to sort it out. I knew right from wrong, and I had done wrong. I wasn't afraid to pay for it. I didn't particularly want to pay for my sins, but I'd lived all my life in Monroe, and in Monroe, we learn that paying for sins is inevitable, unpleasant though that may be.

But there was another side to the question. I suspected that going to trial would be really hard on the others. And if we admitted we knew about the robbery in advance, that could make it harder for Billy. And C.J. was a terrible old man and deserved to pay for his sins as much as we did. Then I heard Billy say, "That's no reason to rob a man."

And then suddenly it was morning.

10

A lot of county prosecutors use their influence to make life easier for relatives who get into trouble. Others bend over backward to make life harder for wayward relatives, so that no one will accuse them of favoritism.

My Uncle Dave steers a middle course. He treats his relatives the same way he treats everyone else. When Pete and I walked into his office on Saturday afternoon, along with Stella, Alison, Ronnie, and George, he treated us all the way he'd treat any dope-crazed gang of thieves and hoodlums.

"This is a terrible thing," he began. "Have you come to confess? I must warn you . . ." He stopped and stared at Pete as if he'd never seen him before. "What's this child doing here?"

"I want to confess, Uncle Dave," Pete said carefully.

Uncle Dave raised his eyes to heaven.

"We thought you might be able to decide the proper course of action," Dad explained. He had come along to advise us. "The parents held a meeting this morning and we decided to let you handle it. I might add," he added, "that Chief of Police Patterson doesn't seem any too anxious to charge the children. But I would assume you've been on the phone to him."

"I have," Uncle Dave admitted. "The action he's taken is satisfactory, as far as it goes. But he hasn't gone far enough. These youngsters have broken the law, and they ought to pay for it."

"I'm paying for it, I can tell you," Alison muttered.

"I believe that was Chief Patterson's intention," Uncle Dave commented. "But I don't entirely hold with informal arrangements. Most parents can't punish their own children properly. They're not capable of it." He paused and looked at each of us in turn. "Each of you has broken the law. Each has admitted his or her guilt to his or her parents. I'm prepared to charge each of you with juvenile delinquency. If you were older, the charge would be conspiracy. That's a most serious charge."

Dad's voice broke the stunned silence that followed. "Are you sure you want to do this, Dave?"

"Let a youngster get away with a crime, and he'll go on to bigger ones," Uncle Dave said. "Now, I know Chief Patterson doesn't agree with me. He cites sociological studies purporting to prove that, if a child breaks the law once and isn't brought to trial, he'll never do it again. He claims that, once a child is branded a lawbreaker, he believes it and breaks the law again and again to prove it. Now I wouldn't know anything about that, but I know the law. I'll have to charge all of you with juvenile delinquency. With the exception of this child," he said, indicating Pete.

"Why not?" Pete asked.

"You weren't a party to the conspiracy," Uncle Dave explained, irritated.

Pete looked disappointed. If the chief's sociological theories were right, Pete would never become a criminal. The rest of us were doomed.

I glanced at Dad while Uncle Dave was telling us more about subpoenas than we wanted to know. To a casual acquaintance, Dad might have looked sad; but I knew him better than that. He was fighting mad.

The subject was dropped for the rest of the weekend, at least in my family. We'd decided not to discuss it. There was not very much to discuss in any case, as far as I could see.

118

There was no wriggling out of Uncle Dave's strict interpretation of the law.

When the lunch bell rang on Monday, Miss Holloway asked the five conspirators to stay behind for a few minutes.

"They're trying to starve us into submission," Ronnie grumbled.

"The lunch line will be past the front entrance by the time we get there," I agreed. "Do you think you'll make it, Stella? Stella?"

Stella didn't answer. She seemed lost in a quiet world of her own.

"I have just heard about the trouble you have got into," Miss Holloway announced. "I am shocked. Surely you all know right from wrong. What have you to say for yourselves?"

"I believe we're being charged in the courts of law, ma'am," Ronnie said.

"And rightly so," Miss Holloway remarked. "Now I'd like you to know that the principal has decided not to suspend you. It was decided that you'd learn more good citizenship in the classroom than out on the streets."

It was the first news we'd heard about suspension. I was beginning to realize what it feels like to be a criminal.

"The principal has asked me to tell you," Miss Holloway continued, "that you are all expected in the county prosecutor's office at four o'clock. You are dismissed for lunch."

"I guess this is when he serves the subpoenas," Alison said.

"I don't see why we have to go and pick them up," Ronnie said. "He's supposed to find us. Why should we save the taxpayers' money?"

"Are we going to go?" George asked.

"I don't see how we can avoid it," Alison said. "Come on, cheer up. The condemned ate a hearty lunch."

We fell in at the end of the line.

119

Stella and I brought up the rear. "Listen," she whispered suddenly. "My mama's left."

"What?" I said, startled.

"Shh," Stella said. "Don't tell nobody. If they find out, they'll make me go live with my Uncle Phil in Atlanta." She shuddered. "You know, the chicken killer. Lord."

"Where did your mama go?" I whispered.

"Miami," Stella said. "She said I could go with her. I told her I couldn't because they're going to charge me. She said they wouldn't send nobody after an insignificant kid like me. Lord, I wouldn't go running off to Miami and leave y'all to take the rap alone."

"Why did she go off like that?" I asked, after a moment.

"It was because of Billy getting caught and all," Stella explained. "She said she wasn't going to let no man ruin her life again, not even her own son. She said he was just trash. Trash," she repeated. "Guess everybody thinks so now."

"Not my Mom," I said, to cheer her up. "She thinks he's a nice guy. Just a little confused."

"Me too," Stella said, and smiled. "Confused, I mean. And condemned, like Alison said."

We picked up our trays.

Word must get around fast, because it seemed half the people in the lunchroom wanted the five of us to share their tables. We chose a table by ourselves, but people kept coming by to say hello and to ask whether we had a good lawyer, and whether C.J. had really pulled a gun, and more dumb questions like that.

Finally, Ronnie burst out in exasperation: "This isn't a joke! We may go to jail. They'll put us on a chain gang."

"They don't put women on chain gangs in the state of Florida," Alison pointed out. "Women work in the prison laundry."

120

I was getting a little disgusted with both of them. Even when Ronnie and Alison took something seriously, they didn't take it seriously enough. "You're both too intellectual," I said finally. "You keep getting bogged down in details."

They both looked at me, startled. "I beg your pardon," I said, and returned to my lunch.

Dad was waiting in Uncle Dave's waiting room when we arrived, and he was grinning to beat the band. "This way, children," he said, opening the door to Uncle Dave's inner office. "The county prosecutor is expecting you."

Uncle Dave looked decidedly depressed.

"It is my duty," he said mournfully, "to tell you that the case against you has been dropped. Mr. Caldwell has declined to press charges."

Stella's voice rang out loud and clear as a bell in the absolute silence that followed this announcement:

"What about Billy?"

"I'm glad to say Mr. Caldwell isn't completely out of touch with reality," Uncle Dave said. "Your brother has been released on bail, but charges have been filed against him. Trespassing and attempted larceny."

No one had the courage to look at Stella. I was staring at Uncle Dave, who suddenly flushed. "You may use my office," he said to Dad, and made a quick exit.

"I don't think there are enough chairs here," Dad said, sitting on the desk. "You may just make yourselves comfortable on this excellent Persian carpet."

We sat on the rug.

"You may know that your parents have been meeting regularly throughout the weekend to straighten out the details of this unhappy affair," Dad said. "You may be sure that whatever I say has been agreed upon in advance by all of us. I'm merely a spokesman for the parents.

"Stella," Dad went on. "We all feel very bad about Billy. The consensus of the parents is that, far from leading you astray, Billy went out of his way to protect you children from the consequences of your criminal natures. We took up a collection and stood bail for Billy."

"Why?" said Stella, startled.

Dad smiled. "It's not every day we get an all-scholastic safety in Monroe. We'd like to keep him."

We all smiled then.

"If Billy leaves town," Dad continued, "bail will be forfeited and we'll lose our money. We're counting on Billy to remain for his trial. You might tell him that."

"Yes, sir," Stella said.

"We don't condone what you children have done," Dad said, "but the charges were completely out of proportion. The only thing you children are guilty of is bad judgment. Billy's problem is far more serious. He's not a minor. If he's convicted, he'll go to prison. George, your mother has been in touch with a criminal lawyer in Miami to represent Billy. The money we've put up for Billy's bond ought to go toward the lawyer's fees."

"Billy will pay you back," Stella put in suddenly.

"We have no doubt," Dad replied. "Now we can pass to the second item on our agenda. We believe you children are entitled to some explanation, if only to know by whose good grace you have managed to escape reform school. I believe that Emily used her influence to induce her father to drop the charges. Are there any questions?"

"What influence, sir?" Ronnie asked.

"It would appear that she has begun to exert considerable influence over her father," Dad replied. "I think we'll find she'll be back in school tomorrow."

"But what happened, sir?" George asked.

"Your parents have delegated me to explain as much of the situation as I see fit," Dad said. "This is as much as I think you ought to know. If your parents want you to know more, I'm sure they'll tell you themselves. Now I suggest you all make your respective ways home and see what penance your parents have cooked up for you. The consensus of the parents this morning was that as the courts will not have the opportunity to punish you, it is up to each of us."

"I think I'd prefer the courts," Alison said.

"I daresay," Dad agreed. He looked at Ronnie. "Your parents had trouble finding a proper punishment, so Mr. and Mrs. Stewart gave them a few ideas. We all felt that the two of you are so alike that what will teach one of you a lesson will teach the other as well."

Ronnie opened his mouth and then shut it again.

"I believe this meeting can be considered over and the affair resolved satisfactorily," Dad said. "Stella, Mrs. Allen has asked you to drop by the house before going home."

"I can't," Stella hissed at me as we bolted out ahead of the others. "Your mama's going to ask me where my mama is. She left last night."

"That's okay," I said. "I'll tell Mom you had homework or something. What do you suppose really happened to make C.J. drop the charges?"

"I don't know and I don't care," Stella said. Her face was the palest I'd ever seen it. "They're gonna put Billy in jail."

"Maybe the lawyer can get him off," I said, trying to cheer her up.

"Mary Frances," Stella said, "you know Billy's guilty. There's nothing no lawyer can do for him."

"Oh, I don't know," I said. "I hear these Miami lawyers are really smart."

Stella gave me a long, desolate look. "Ain't nobody good enough to save Billy," she said, and ran down the stairs.

I watched her go. Ronnie, George, and Alison caught up with me, and we stood at the top of the stairs, listening to the street door open and shut.

"I don't think there's anything we can do to help her, Mary Frances," Alison said.

"If George's mom's picked a lawyer," Ronnie added, "he's the best in the state."

George's mother is secretary to old Judge Harris, George's grandfather. The judge isn't the only lawyer in Monroe, but he's certainly the most successful one.

"I guess your mom knows every lawyer in the state of Florida," I said hopefully.

"I wouldn't say that," George said. "The thing that bothers me is that Mom and Grandfather don't know anything about criminal law. All they know about is trusts and estates."

George is ignorant in a number of subjects, but he knows as much about the law as he knows about medicine. The reason is the same: he's grown up with it. He tends to forget that the rest of us haven't.

"What's trusts and estates?" I asked.

"In layman's terms," he said, "that means wills. An estate is composed of the real and tangible property a person leaves when he dies."

"I see," I said. I decided not to ask what a trust was.

"A trust," George went on, "is more complicated."

"I wouldn't be surprised," I said. "What do you suppose made C.J. change his mind?"

"Huh?"

"You know," I said. "About charging us."

"I don't think we've been told as much as we ought to know," Alison said.

"I don't believe they're going to tell us, either," Ronnie said. "But it's pretty obvious, isn't it?"

"Not to me," I said.

124

Ronnie draped his arm across my shoulders. "Mary Frances," he said, "when the children of the town's leading families get into trouble, what do you think happens?"

"We're not the town's leading families," I objected.

"Well, my family isn't." Ronnie grinned. "Nor is Stella's family. But the Harrises are. Sorry, George. And in their way, so are the Stewarts and the Allens, Mary Frances. Your parents and George's parents and mine all went to school with each other, and with the chief of police, and with half the officials in Monroe. Our parents all go to the same church. They belong to the same clubs. When a man runs for office in this town, it's like running for class president. The most popular fellow wins."

"I can't believe my parents would try to influence the course of justice," Alison said.

"Maybe they didn't," Ronnie said. "And maybe they did. If they did, they'll never admit it to us. It's something we'll never be able to prove."

The door to Uncle Dave's office opened. Dad strode briskly through the door into the hall. He stopped when he spotted us huddled at the top of the stairs.

"I think it may be a good idea if you children dispersed," he said. "The county prosecutor is in an unhappy state of mind." He grinned. "He may charge you with loitering."

We dispersed.

Under ordinary circumstances, Ronnie, George, Alison, and I formed a loose and casual group. We had been the best of friends for years, but that didn't mean we stuck together like glue. We drifted in and out of each other's lives, depending on our moods. Sometimes two or three of us ate lunch together, for example; on other days, we didn't. Sometimes we met after school; on other days, we had other things to do.

Stella drifted into our group the day we met her. She was

as casual as the rest of us. Most days, likely as not, she'd decide to eat lunch in privacy in a corner of the cafeteria, or walk home alone along a private and solitary route.

But in the days that followed the attempted robbery, the five of us found ourselves together nearly all the time. For one thing, we wanted to avoid the stupid questions people were sure to ask us, so we avoided people altogether. And we had a lot to discuss.

Stella was a depressing companion. Walking home from school, she'd close into herself, and at lunchtime, she sat pale and silent, sipping her milk.

George shot Stella an uneasy glance the day after the meeting in Uncle Dave's office as he banged his tray down on the table and eased into a chair next to Alison. He was so nervous he bit off half his hamburger in one go, chewed it manfully, and washed it down noisily with half his Coke. He didn't take his eyes off Stella.

He wasn't the only one. Ronnie and Alison kept glancing at Stella as well.

I understood the problem. We were all out of danger, and we felt guilty about it. Billy was going to jail while we all had got off scot-free.

But understanding the problem didn't make the atmosphere any less oppressive. I decided to do something about it.

"George," I said.

He looked up, startled. "Mary Frances," he boomed.

"George," I said. "Is there something you want to tell us?"

George shot Stella another uneasy glance. She was gazing toward the window.

"Don't worry about it," I said, hoping George would understand.

He did. He looked away from Stella and plunged into his story.

"I think I know why C.J. changed his mind," he said. "It's got something to do with a will."

"A will!" I echoed. "What gives you that idea?"

"Mom," George said simply.

"I guess your mom ought to know, if anybody does," Ronnie said, tearing his gaze away from Stella. "Who left a will?"

"Mrs. C.J."

We digested the information in silence.

Ronnie and Alison began gazing at Stella.

"Funny, Mrs. C.J. went to your grandfather to make a will," I said hastily.

"Where else would she go?" said Alison, her attention distracted. "Everybody goes to Judge Harris. Can you think of another lawyer who draws up wills?"

"No," I admitted. "Actually, I can't even think of another lawyer."

"Why," Alison said, warming to her subject, "my parents went to Judge Harris when they made their wills."

"Did your parents make a will?"

"Certainly," Alison said. "I suppose your parents have made wills too."

"It's a good idea to make a will," George said. "It makes a lot of problems for a family if a person dies intestate."

I was afraid George was going to tell us what "intestate" meant, but Alison didn't give him the chance.

"No," she said, "I'm not surprised Mrs. C.J. went to Judge Harris. I'm just surprised she had anything to leave."

A part of my penance consisted of occupying myself in a constructive fashion. In practical terms, that meant turning up in the kitchen at 4:45 every afternoon, sitting at the table, and peeling potatoes.

I decided to take advantage of the situation that same

afternoon. I'd peeled four potatoes before I took the plunge.

"If Mrs. C.J. made a will," I asked Mom suddenly, "what would she have to leave?"

Mom whirled around to stare at me. To my annoyance, she stared at the potatoes I'd peeled instead.

"There's more potato on the floor than on the table," Mom said. "You could try to peel them a little more carefully. You know all the goodness in potatoes is concentrated just under the skin."

"Yes, ma'am," I said, and Mom turned back to the sink.

I peeled another potato. Then I tried again.

"I suppose the house belonged to Mrs. C.J."

"No," Mom replied. "C.J. built the house."

"With his own hands?"

"Of course not," Mom said. "They hired a contractor."

I peeled another potato.

"Stocks and bonds?"

"I don't think so."

"What else is there?" I asked. "The store?"

Mom didn't answer at once. She came over to the table and sat across from me. She picked up a peeled potato. "I don't think they'd take you in the Army."

"Did Mrs. C.J. own the store?"

"I believe she did," Mom said. "I'm going to tell you about it because I think you may learn something from it." She paused. "When Callie ran off at the age of sixteen to marry a man with no resources, she wasn't thinking ahead. They came back to Monroe, and six months later neither of them had found a job. Well, neither of them was trained to do any kind of work, and jobs were scarce in Monroe at the time. They were singularly lacking in imagination. They didn't think of trying to work in the fields. They set up a tent in the park and slowly starved. One day C.J. walked into the hospital carrying Callie in his arms. She had a severe case of malnutrition and was so weak she couldn't walk. C.J. admitted that they ate one day out of every two, and their meals were pitiful indeed."

Mom gazed out the window. Then she turned back to me. "Callie's father was not a poor man. We all wondered why she didn't ask him for help. She had asked him, in the beginning. But Mr. Randolph, her father, had turned her down. He was so angry when she married C.J. that he said he was willing to let her starve."

"What about welfare?"

"It's difficult to get welfare here," Mom said. "It always has been. Monroe is dedicated to the work ethic." I looked up, surprised at the bitterness in her voice. For a moment, she'd sounded like Emily.

"How did they buy the store?"

"Well, when Mr. Randolph found his daughter well and truly starving to death, he relented. He agreed to buy Callie and C.J. a modest business of their choice. They chose to run a grocery store." Mom smiled. "Callie once told me that they chose the store so they'd never starve again. If things went bad, they could just eat up the stock."

"Mr. Randolph made one condition," Mom continued. "He insisted on putting everything in Callie's name. He knew his daughter to be foolish, and he thought it would offer her some protection. The store and the land were leased in her name. The business is incorporated, and that's in her name as well. Poor Callie. She never did take advantage of the situation." Mom fixed me with a steely look. "And that is what happens to young girls who quit school to marry worthless boys with no money and no prospects."

"I'm not quitting school," I said hastily. "Nobody wants to marry me, anyway."

"I'm not surprised," Mom said. "Judging by the way you peel potatoes, Ronnie would do better to look after his own dinner."

"Who said anything about Ronnie?" I said quickly. I tried clenching my fists the way Billy did. It helped.

Mom returned to the sink. I gathered the peelings off the floor and threw them into the compost bucket. We don't have a garden, but Mom collects peelings for a gardening family down the block. My penance included weeding their garden on weekends. I wasn't looking forward to it.

"Did Mrs. C.J. leave the store to C.J.?" I asked finally.

"She left the store to Emily," Mom said.

I sat at the table. "So she did take advantage of the situation."

"Emily's a bright young lady," Mom said. "When she finds an advantage like that, she knows how to use it. You ought to be grateful to her. She used it on your behalf."

"I don't know," Alison remarked the next day at lunch. "I think it must be more than that, although I admit it gives her some bargaining power. If Emily owns the store, she can run it the way she likes. She can hire a boy and go back to school."

"Not yet," George pointed out. "She's still a minor. Grandfather is acting as her guardian in business matters until she's eighteen."

"Your grandfather's on her side," Ronnie argued. "He'd probably agree to anything she wanted to do with the store."

"If Emily owns the store," I said, "she can cut off C.J.'s income just like that."

"What about the gas pump?" Alison said. "C.J.'s pretty proud of that franchise. That must belong to him."

We pondered the question in silence.

"I know this isn't very tactful," Alison said suddenly, "but I think we ought to talk about it. I don't know whether Emily got us out of trouble or whether it was our parents, as Ronnie said."

"How can you doubt me?" Ronnie asked cheerfully.

"Shut up, Ronnie," Alison said. "What bothers me is that nobody seems able to do anything for Billy."

Stella lifted her head and gazed at Alison.

"Stella, you know it's not fair," Alison said. "Billy didn't rob that store. He only tried to rob it. And you know we're as guilty as he is. Our intentions were as criminal as his."

"They tried," Stella said.

"I beg your pardon?" I asked.

"They tried," Stella repeated, her mouth set in a bitter line. "Your folks did all they could, far as I know. They talked to C.J., anyway. Emily talked to C.J. Even that Miami lawyer talked to C.J."

"I don't get it," I said. "Does C.J. really hate Billy that much?"

"It isn't C.J.," Stella said. "It's Billy."

George leaned over Ronnie and touched Stella's arm to get her attention. "Isn't Billy going to accept the offer?" he boomed in what he obviously thought was a whisper.

"I guess so," Stella replied.

"What offer?" I asked.

"Billy's going to cop a plea," Stella said dully.

George beamed at me. "I guess you don't know what that means, Mary Frances."

"Got it," I replied.

"It's also called plea bargaining," George explained. "The defendant pleads guilty to a lesser charge, and the prosecution agrees to drop the more serious charge."

"What you're saying is that Billy's going to plead guilty to trespassing," Ronnie said, "and C.J. will drop the charge of attempted larceny."

"That's right," George said. "Billy came by the house last night to tell us. Mom was sure glad she retained that Miami lawyer. It was his idea. Seems they do it all the time in Miami."

"Well, that's not so bad," Alison said. I could hear the relief in her voice. "Billy won't get a very long sentence for trespassing."

"Ten days to a month," George said. "It's usually ten days. He can serve it right here in Monroe. He'd go to the county jail instead of a state prison."

"Billy's a fool," Stella said bitterly. "He didn't have to go to jail at all." She stood up so abruptly that her chair tipped over. She stared at it a moment and then turned and ran out of the lunchroom.

11

I was drying a dinner plate that night when the doorbell rang, and I was so startled that I dropped it. The plate hit the floor and shattered into several uneven pieces and a fair amount of fine china dust.

"Of course, we could use paper plates until your penance has expired," Mom said sadly.

"Would you like me to answer the door?"

"I'm sure your father will see to that," Mom said. "Why don't you fetch a broom and clean that up?"

Dad appeared in the doorway a minute later.

"Are you free, Margaret?" Dad asked Mom. "Billy and Emily have dropped by to talk to us."

"Yes, of course," Mom said, drying her soapy hands. "I've just finished. Mary Frances, why don't you take that pitcher of iced tea out of the refrigerator? Oh, dear," she said, and winced.

"Are you all right, Margaret?" Dad asked.

"Yes, perfectly," Mom said. "I suddenly had a nightmare vision of Mary Frances balancing a tray of glasses from here to the living room. I'll ask Emily to lend a hand. Now don't you carry anything breakable, Mary Frances," Mom said sternly, and swept out of the kitchen.

Emily appeared as I was sweeping up the broken plate.

"Evening, Mary Frances," she said. "Where does your mother keep the glasses?"

Emily had a tray prepared with glasses and a pitcher of iced tea by the time I'd disposed of the broken plate. We marched single file into the living room.

Billy was sitting in the chair his mother had occupied the first time he'd come to the house. Pete was standing behind him. My parents were sitting on the couch, leaning forward attentively.

"Ah," Mom said. "Thank you, Emily. If you youngsters would just help yourselves."

"I'll be glad to serve," Emily said. "You can go ahead and explain, Billy."

"Right," Billy said. "I thought I ought to tell you what I've decided to do and why I'm doing it. I feel I owe you that much. I owe you a good deal more, sir."

Dad looked embarrassed. "You don't owe us anything."

"I'm sorry to have to contradict you, sir," Billy went on. "My family has lived in more than a dozen towns since I was born. We've never stayed in a place long enough to get to know anyone very well. I've been in trouble before," he said, and stopped.

Emily was handing Mom a glass of iced tea and her hand paused in midair. She turned and looked at Billy.

"Billy," she said, "Mr. and Mrs. Allen know you've been in trouble before. Don't be so sensitive."

"I've been in trouble before, as you know," Billy said, and smiled. "Nobody we knew would lift a finger to help. You people have been a revelation to me. I've never met people so kind and good-hearted. I guess that's why I don't mind going to jail." He paused. "I guess you've heard I'm making a deal."

"We had heard something to that effect," Dad admitted.

"I'll be going to jail on the trespassing charge," Billy went on. "My lawyer tells me there's nothing wrong with plea bargaining. It's efficient and merciful, and it saves the taxpayers

134

the cost of a trial. But I want you to know I would never have agreed if I'd been guilty to start with."

"I don't understand, Billy," Mom said.

"You don't explain things as well as you might do, Billy," Emily said, handing Billy his iced tea. She sat cross-legged at his feet. Billy set his glass on the floor and grabbed Emily's hand.

"I'll try to explain, ma'am," he said to Mom. "When I went to C.J.'s store, I intended to rob it. I can't deny that. I had criminal intentions. But when I reached the cold case, I discovered I couldn't do it. I remember stretching my hand out toward the loose brick in back and then pulling my hand away. I knew I couldn't do it."

"Why not?" Pete asked suddenly.

Billy twisted around to look at him. "I thought about that, Pete," he said. "It's not good for a man to be a criminal. It's not a good way to live." He turned back to Mom and Dad. "And then," he grinned, "it occurred to me that I'd never be able to explain it to Emily. She'd make me give the money back."

"Billy was just turning away from the cold case when Papa caught him," Emily said. "Papa admitted it to me, night before last. Can you imagine the wickedness of that man? He was ready to send Billy to jail, and he knew Billy was innocent. Papa hasn't heard the last of this."

"I daresay he hasn't," Dad said, smiling. He picked up his iced tea.

"I don't want to appear dense," Mom said, "but I still don't understand why you're going to jail at all."

Dad set his iced tea back on the coffee table, untasted. "I must say I don't quite understand either."

"You really don't explain things very well, Billy," Emily said.

"I suppose I don't," Billy admitted. "Well, now, I'm going

to jail for trespassing because I'm guilty of that. I was trespassing, all right. C.J. didn't invite me into his store."

"I'm sure the judge will suspend your sentence, Billy," Dad said.

"He might," Billy agreed, "but I doubt it. The county prosecutor will see to that." He smiled. "I don't mind going to jail, sir. I've told my lawyer not to press very hard for a suspended sentence."

"Why on earth not?" Mom asked.

"Two reasons, ma'am. Or maybe they're both the same." He leaned back in the chair, as if he'd finished speaking.

"Billy!" Emily said, exasperated.

Billy straightened up again. "I usually explain things more coherently," he said. "Maybe I'm nervous." He glanced at Emily. "I want to make some kind of gesture. This is a good town, and there are good people here. I like Monroe well enough to make my life here. I want to start out on the right foot, to put my past behind me. When I walk out of the jail two weeks from now, it will be like starting a new life."

"But, Billy," Mom protested, "you don't have to go that far."

"I think I do, ma'am," Billy said. "The kids I've met are a fine bunch of kids, but their attitude toward life seems a little slapdash. I figure I'm doing it for Mary Frances," he said, looking at me. "For Pete. For Ronnie and George and Alison, and particularly for Stella. I want to show these kids that it isn't a joke to break the law. It's just a gesture, but it's something I feel I have to do. They might learn something from it."

Mom and Dad gazed at Billy, completely speechless.

"You might say Billy's a volunteer object lesson," Emily said dryly. "Personally, I think he's crazy. Billy, you were going to ask about Stella."

"Right," Billy replied. "I suppose you folks know Mama's taking a little vacation."

136

"No," Mom said. "I had no idea."

"There's no way of knowing when she'll be back," Billy went on. "I don't think I'd feel easy leaving Stella alone in that big house. She's a strange girl. She hasn't had an easy life. And she's spent too much time alone. When she's hurt or unhappy, she closes up. I guess you've noticed that, Mary Frances."

I admitted that I had.

"She's going to be very hurt and unhappy when I go to jail," Billy went on. "She's got the idea I could have my sentence suspended, and she's furious that I won't even try." He paused and stared at the floor. Then he looked back at my parents. "Stella's different from the kids I've met here. I guess you could say she's more intense. She's capable of looking after herself, but I don't feel easy leaving her alone at a time like this. I was wondering if you'd be kind enough to take her in for a few days."

"Why, of course," Mom said. "It will be our pleasure."

"Stella can stay with us as long as she likes," Dad added. "When do you think you'll be checking into Chief Patterson's modern new jailhouse, Billy?"

"We're seeing the judge tomorrow," Billy said. "There won't be a trial because I'm pleading guilty to the only charge still lodged against me. I'd like to go in day after tomorrow and get my sentence over with before Christmas. Of course, it's not up to me."

"The sooner Billy goes in, the sooner he's out," Emily said cheerfully. She lifted her glass. "Shall we drink to Billy's new life?" She took a sip of her iced tea and looked up, startled.

"Is something wrong, Emily?" Dad asked.

"Oh, no, sir," Emily said hastily.

Dad sipped his iced tea. He set the glass carefully down on the coffee table.

"Margaret," he said. "Have you allowed Mary Frances to prepare the refreshments?"

Mom looked guilty. "The poor child," she said. "I don't want to give her a complex."

"Just what did you put into this iced tea, Mary Frances?" Dad asked. "I assume this was intended to be iced tea."

"Tea," I said. "Lemon. Sugar. Cocoa."

"Cocoa?" Dad said. "Cocoa?"

"I thought I'd be a little creative."

"I like it," Pete said suddenly.

I leaped from my chair and hugged him. Pete looked at me as if I'd gone crazy. I suppose I had. But I had to hug somebody.

"If I compliment your iced tea, Mary Frances, will you hug me too?" Billy asked.

"Try it," I said boldly.

Billy took a sip of his iced tea. He set it down again. "Gee, Mary Frances, I'd like to . . ." Billy began.

Mom, Dad and Emily started to laugh. I decided to clench my fists.

Billy stood up slowly. "I've had a lot of iced tea in my time," he said, "but I've never tasted anything like that." And he hugged me.

Stella moved in two days later.

Ronnie came by on Monday to talk about algebra, but Stella didn't even say hello. She glanced at him, walked into my bedroom, and shut the door.

"She's really taking it hard," Ronnie remarked.

"Yes," I agreed. "She's real pleasant to be around."

Ronnie looked at me sharply. "How would you like it if Pete went to jail?"

"But Billy doesn't mind," I pointed out.

"Mary Frances," Ronnie said, "when people do things for their own reasons, people might understand their motives, but they don't have to like it."

"What are you talking about?"

"I'm not sure," Ronnie said. "Let's see what you can do with this one. If X equals forty . . ."

Mom and Dad decided Stella should share my penance, as long as she was sharing my room. In practical terms, that meant Stella got to cook while I had to peel potatoes. I noticed that Stella cheered up when Mom let her baste the roast beef or cook the string beans. On the day they iced the chocolate cake, Stella finally smiled.

Stella melted the chocolate, beat in the sugar and egg whites, and swirled the frosting in great showy sweeps around the top and sides of the cake. I sat brooding at the kitchen table, peeling potatoes.

"Can Mary Frances put the cherries on, ma'am?" Stella asked suddenly.

Mom looked at me critically.

That's when Stella smiled.

"I don't think she'll hurt it," Stella said, "just putting a few cherries on top."

Mom made one last effort to avoid certain disaster. "The cherries ought to go on immediately, before the frosting hardens," she said, "and Mary Frances has to feed the dogs."

"I can feed the dogs," Stella said.

"Well, all right," Mom said, giving in. "I'll lend a hand. Now I don't think you have to cover the top of the cake with cherries, Mary Frances," Mom said. "Half a dozen ought to do it."

"Any special design, ma'am?" I asked sarcastically.

Mom doesn't understand sarcasm. "Oh, no," she answered seriously. "Be creative."

Mom and Stella bustled around the kitchen, opening dog-food bags and emptying them into the washtub.

"Where's Scrappy's bowl?" Stella asked.

Mom fetched the bowl and Stella filled it. Then Stella picked up the washtub and the two of them disappeared into the yard.

Stella returned a moment later, dragging Scrappy by the collar. "Here you go," she said, and put his bowl down on the floor.

We watched him dig in. "Poor little guy," Stella said. She sat cross-legged on the floor, across the bowl from Scrappy. "Poor little guy," she said again.

Scrappy lifted his head from the bowl and stared at Stella. She didn't move. He stuck his nose back into the bowl and finished his dinner. Then he looked at Stella again.

"You don't have to eat so fast," Stella said. "Nobody's going to take your dinner away."

Scrappy stuck his front paw in the empty bowl and wagged his tail.

"You're welcome," Stella said politely, as Mom opened the screen door, the empty washtub in her hand. Scrappy bolted out into the yard.

Mom looked hard at Stella. "That dog seems to like you," she said. "I don't suppose . . ." She stopped.

"What don't you suppose?" I asked.

"We'll see," Mom said. "Let's see what you've done with the cake, Mary Frances."

There isn't much you can do with six cherries. I'd placed them in a circle.

"Why, that's wonderful, Mary Frances," Mom said. "It looks very festive."

"It was nothing," I said modestly.

"I think you may be coming along," Mom said, smiling at me.

Stella's mood lifted steadily. On the morning of the day Billy's sentence was due to end, she actually whistled as she packed her suitcase.

"I'll take all this home on the way to school," Stella said. "Meet you in half an hour by C.J.'s." And she disappeared.

Stella was waiting on the corner when I arrived.

"Everything's spic and span," she said. "I bet Billy's home when I come back from school."

"Do you think so?"

"You never know," Stella said cheerily, and we walked to school.

Stella couldn't sit still in class. Miss Holloway called on her once, and Stella leaped to her feet and shouted the answer. After that, Miss Holloway decided to ignore her.

Ronnie didn't. "What's going on?" he asked me in the lunch line.

"Billy's coming home today," I told him.

"Of course," Ronnie said. "I wasn't thinking. Has her mother come back?"

"I don't think so."

"What if Billy isn't there when she gets home?" Ronnie asked.

"I don't want to think about it."

"I guess she'll be upset."

"Ronnie," I said, "Stella's so happy right now that if anything happens to upset her, she'll go to pieces."

We'd reached the front of the line. Ronnie picked up his tray, slid it along the counter, and picked up three hamburgers. He handed one to me.

"I think I'll just wander along to C.J.'s this afternoon for a Nehi," he said casually.

That's how Ronnie and I happened to be along when Stella left school that afternoon. Ronnie wheeled his bike while I ran to keep up with Stella.

"Do you think he'll want a steak?" Stella asked me.

"I don't know."

"I bet he'd like a steak," she said. "Do you think he'll look any different?"

"I don't know."

"I bet he'll look different."

The conversation was depressing me. Then it took a turn for the worse.

"When Papa died," Stella said, "Mama cried for a week. She went straight to bed and cried for a week. I thought she'd never stop. I couldn't stand it. I went off into the swamp, just to find me a little peace and quiet. Billy came and got me. He said he and Mama, they needed me."

She suddenly bolted ahead. I looked up and spotted Billy, standing on the corner of Second Street a block away and waving to beat the band.

I think Stella ran that block in thirty seconds flat. Billy picked her up and swung her around and around, a foot off the ground. He set her down at arm's length and looked at her, and then he put his arm around her and they started up Second Street.

"I don't see what all the fuss was about," Ronnie growled.

"You know," I said, "I think maybe she was afraid he wasn't coming back. Nobody else ever did. Her father died and her mother's run off to Miami. . . ." I stopped.

Ronnie shot me a long and searching look. "For somebody who can't understand algebra," he said, "you seem to have a lot of opinions."

"That's not very tactful."

"Come on, kid," Ronnie said. "I'll buy you a Nehi. Unless you want to stand here talking all day."

12

The last day of January dawned bright and clear. It always has. The principal considers it some kind of sign, because the first school term ends on the last day of January. I believe the principal enjoys that day more than any other —except for the day that ends the second school term.

At two o'clock on the last day of January, the entire Monroe School student body filed into the auditorium for the semi-annual End of Term Assembly.

The principal looked positively jovial as he stepped onto the stage.

"I'm pleased to say that all of you passed the term," he began. "However, some of you just squeaked by. You know which ones you are." He peered significantly at the audience.

"This has not been a bad term," he continued. "The weather has held. You students have not staged any protests. Our football team has given a good account of itself, rising to second place in the division. Let's hear it for the team."

The audience cheered.

"Wait till next year!" the principal shouted, and the audience cheered again.

The principal continued. "Our crime wave seems to have burned itself out," he said. "I undertand the youngsters involved have decided to behave themselves. Although I hear there was a bank robbery in Miami day before yesterday, heh, heh."

The audience laughed dutifully.

"And now for the prizes," the principal said.

He disappeared into the wings and returned pushing a wheelbarrow stacked with prizes and trophies.

"There seem to be more prizes than ever this year," the principal said. "As you may know, these prizes are donated by the Junior Chamber of Commerce to give you youngsters added incentive to bring credit upon yourselves, your school, and your fine city. Let's hear it for the Junior Chamber of Commerce."

The audience cheered.

"Now let me see." The principal fumbled among the trophies. "Here we are. Best all-around quarterback of the year. I can't seem to read the name."

He squinted at the trophy. The audience tittered.

"Oh, yes, there it is. Why, it's Ronnie Bean."

The audience cheered as Ronnie trotted up to accept his trophy.

And so it continued. There were trophies for the best girl athlete and the best school-crossing guard. The best student in the Spanish class won a record; the top history student got a book about the War Between the States; the best musician in the school band won a metronome. There must have been a dozen trophies and prizes in all.

At the end there were only a couple of books left in the wheelbarrow.

"I bet those are for the maps," I whispered to Stella.

The principal confirmed my guess. "I understand there was a mapmaking contest in Miss Holloway's class," he said. "Miss Holloway has asked me to announce that all the maps were excellent, although some, of course, were better than others. These two remaining prizes are for originality in map-making. Stella Shanks and Mary Frances Allen."

Stella leaped to her feet. I had never seen a bigger smile on her face. It was just a prize, after all, but by the time Stella reached the stage she was glowing.

My prize was a paperback atlas, which seemed suitable for the occasion. Stella's prize was a one-volume encyclopedia.

Stella stood transfixed and smiling. "Come on," I whispered, and pulled her off the stage.

She had the book open by the time we'd climbed down from the stage. I had to lead her back to her seat while she leafed through the book. She studied the book through the rest of the assembly and only closed it when we went back to Miss Holloway's room to pick up our report cards.

"Did you know the Allegheny is a river in Pennsylvania?" she asked me as we strolled out into the crisp January sunshine.

"No, I didn't."

"It's also part of the Appalachian Mountain chain," Stella went on. "The Allegheny mountains extend from Pennsylvania to Virginia."

"I didn't know that."

"I bet you don't know what the galaxy is."

"Isn't that a group of stars and planets?"

"You're right," she replied. "I guess everything worth knowing is right here in this fine book."

We walked along in silence.

"You know," Stella said, "I never thought I'd win a prize for anything. I'm not real smart and I'm sure not pretty. But I got a prize for originality. I guess that makes me original."

We laughed.

"It makes me original too," I reminded her. "We both won."

"Yeah," Stella said. "I guess you're used to winning prizes."

"Well, no, not exactly," I admitted. "This is the first one."

"No kidding," Stella said. "Let's stop by C.J.'s. Billy's going to be proud."

C.J. was sitting out on his bench, a half-empty bottle of beer in his hand.

"Afternoon, C.J.," Stella said.

C.J. glared at us. "Go on, git inside," he said finally. "Your brother's waiting on you."

Billy was standing behind the counter. He'd tied on a butcher's smock. He smiled at us. "Is school over already? Did you pass?"

"Better than that," Stella said. "Just look at this. Show him your book, Mary Frances."

We laid our books out on the counter.

"We were awarded first prize in original mapmaking," Stella explained.

"Fantastic," Billy said. He opened the encyclopedia. Then he leafed through the atlas.

"First-rate books," Billy said. "This calls for a celebration. Stella, why don't you fetch a couple of orange sodas."

Stella strolled over to the cold case.

Billy reached into his pocket and pulled out twenty cents. He rang up the amount on the cash register and dropped the change into the drawer.

"Do you have to pay for your own sodas, Billy?" I asked.

"I've put this store on a businesslike basis," Billy said. "If the manager starts taking home food without paying for it, this store will never show a decent profit. Those eggs and peanut butter Stella takes home are paid for out of my salary. It's time this store was run according to sound business practices."

He grinned. "C.J. complained in the beginning about paying for his beers, but we worked out a compromise. He pays the wholesale price—but he pays, every time."

Stella returned with the orange sodas.

"Got a letter from Mama," Billy said casually.

146

Stella put her soda down carefully on the counter. "What did she say, Billy?"

"I left it on your bureau."

Stella leaned across the counter. Her voice rose. "But what did she say, Billy?"

Billy glanced at his sister. "She says she's getting along very well. The plan suits her fine. You just send her your report cards, special delivery, and she'll sign them and send them back. It was kind of your mother to suggest it, Mary Frances. Now if Stella stays out of trouble there's no way anyone will find out Mama's gone."

Billy walked around the counter and put his arm around Stella's shoulder.

"You know Mama's coming back," he said gently, "soon as she gets all this out of her system. She won't let them send you to Uncle Phil." He squeezed her tight and then released her and walked back behind the counter. "Oh, yes," he added. "Mama says she'll send us money if we're not getting enough to eat."

"I was forgetting," I suddenly remembered. "Mom said to remind you about coming over for dinner tonight."

"Why don't we go over right now," Stella said, in a strange, angry voice.

"Listen," I said, annoyed. "If you think you're going to do all the fancy things while I have to sit there scraping the carrots all day. . . ."

"Your mama lets you scrape the carrots?" Stella asked, surprised.

"Yeah, I've advanced," I said. "Some days Mom even lets me drop the plastic sack of frozen peas into the boiling water."

Stella laughed. Billy grinned. I glared at both of them.

"Don't forget to feed the dog before you go, Stella," Billy said. "I probably won't have time to go home."

"Of course I won't forget to feed the dog," Stella said. She placed our empty bottles in a rack, and I picked up the books.

"Do you think your mother's ever coming back?" I asked Stella as we walked down Second Street.

"I don't know," she said. "Billy doesn't think so, whatever he says. He thinks she'd be better off staying in Miami. He says she's a free spirit. Him and me, we're different. We like to settle down in a place. But Mama, she's got to be free." Stella stopped and looked at me challengingly. "There are lots of people like their freedom. Nothing wrong with that."

"I didn't say there was," I said. "You're looking pretty moody suddenly."

"Yeah," Stella said. A moment later, she grinned. "Hope Scrappy lets you into my house."

"Why shouldn't he let me into your house?"

"He's a real loyal dog," Stella said. "You know, that dog, he sleeps out in the hall, exactly halfway between my room and Billy's room. Billy measured the distance. Never saw a dog so smart."

Scrappy barked his head off and wagged his tail to beat the band when we climbed the steps to Stella's front porch. He greeted both of us and then followed Stella into the kitchen. He sat patiently while Stella opened a can of dog food and emptied it into a bowl, and then he ate it slowly and casually, pausing now and again to wag his tail.

Stella changed the water in Scrappy's bowl. Then she picked her book up from the kitchen counter.

"I know just the place for this fine book."

I followed her into her room, where she set the book carefully on the rickety table.

"Okay," she said. "Let's go."

We were going out the screen door when Stella stopped. "Wait a minute," she said. "I forgot something." She disappeared down the hall and into her room.

She returned a couple of minutes later and we turned in the general direction of my house.

"John Adams," she said suddenly.

"I beg your pardon?"

"John Adams," Stella repeated. "That's how the second President was called."

"I didn't know that."

We walked on a way.

"Thomas Jefferson," Stella said. "James Madison."

"Your conversation is fascinating."

We started to laugh.

"James Monroe," Stella said, and we walked down the road, laughing like a pair of fools.